THE PLAYS OF

THE PLAYS OF
HAROLD PINTER

An Assessment

by

SIMON TRUSSLER

LONDON
VICTOR GOLLANCZ LTD
1973

ISBN 0 575 00723 0

Printed in Great Britain by
The Camelot Press Ltd, London and Southampton

To
ANNA AND NICHOLAS

Contents

Acknowledgements

For permission to reprint extracts from the plays of Harold Pinter I am indebted to the author and Eyre Methuen Ltd, to whose latest editions of the plays page references in the text are keyed. My thanks are due also to Martin Esslin, who kindly let me see an early proof of his study of Pinter's plays, *The Peopled Wound*, from which I have drawn additional factual information for my own Chronology, and discovered the existence of several unpublished interviews with Pinter. Giles Gordon of Victor Gollancz Ltd has, as ever, been a tactful and tolerant critic, and Carol Murphy a typist applying creative intelligence to my own illegibility.

INTRODUCTION

Introduction

MORE RUBBISH HAS been written about Harold Pinter than all his contemporaries put together. And this is in spite of Pinter's own occasional side-swipes at his more ingenious apologists—attacks, made more in sorrow than in anger, that are the more telling for their rarity. The myth-making is given a good chance to ossify before Pinter transforms yet another red herring into a wet fish—or, as it might be, a weasel into a red herring:

> Once, many years ago, I found myself engaged uneasily in a public discussion on the theatre. Someone asked me what my work was "about". I replied with no thought at all and merely to frustrate this line of enquiry: "The weasel under the cocktail cabinet." That was a great mistake. Over the years I have seen that remark quoted in a number of learned columns. It has now seemingly acquired a profound significance, and is seen to be a highly relevant and meaningful observation about my own work. But for me the remark meant precisely nothing. Such are the dangers of speaking in public.[1]

Such, too, it must be conceded, are the dangers of writing plays in which there's certainly *something* concealing itself under *something*, if it's only a lot of fluff and dust blowing about and getting up critical noses.

And so commentators have tended to pounce upon Pinter's plays like so many crossword-puzzle enthusiasts, dissatisfied till they have found a solution which accords with the compiler's clues down and clues across—a solution likely to be full of words for which the layman has to turn in despair to his dictionary. I won't claim that I've altogether resisted such temptations: but I've tried hard to remember that what we are talking about are vividly *dramatised* actions, intended for performance upon a very solid stage by real live human beings before live audiences—at least some of whose members won't be able to tell an uroboros from an omphalos, or a Rembrandtesque technique of chiaroscuro from an exfoliation of existential givens.[2]

Now it may be that in a desperate attempt to avoid such over-elaboration I have indulged occasionally in the equal and opposite sin of over-simplification. Indeed, in splitting up Harold Pinter's plays into the five chronological categories which form the main chapters of this book I have inevitably thrown suspicion upon the categoriser. But the labels attached to these chapters do, I would argue, suggest dominant thematic concerns traceable to successive periods of Pinter's career. He has almost always been concerned rather with elaborating a dramatic image than with sustaining a developing action—and because his plays thus tend to be lyrical rather than sequential in structure, reach-me-down descriptions can even suggest answers instead of begging questions. Such summing-up of Pinter's plays in shorthand fashion is, at least, less misleading than analysing into the ground his distinctive manner of warping idiomatic English —an occupation in which the need to put what is pinteresque on paper before what is, necessarily, *picturesque* on a stage too often proves overwhelming.

But let me justify the wordplay in that last sentence. What

matters is not that Pinter is an idiosyncratic writer, but whether the sum of his idiosyncrasies produces viable works of theatrical art or merely a piling-up of predictably ambiguous playscripts into a printed canon. Too much time has been spent on academic exegesis of Pinter *merely* because his plays are complex—as if complexity were a virtue in itself. What needs to be examined is why that complexity contributes to making *The Caretaker* a great play and *The Homecoming*, for my money, an intellectualised melodrama which is not ambiguous in any purposeful sense, just arbitrarily enigmatic. Usually, what determines Pinter's worthwhile work from his occasional failures is precisely the ability to fuse personal mannerisms into a satisfactory form *for the stage*: and so, on the few occasions in the pages that follow where I have myself described something as "pinteresque", it is to suggest the tendency towards self-parody to which Pinter has at times been prone, not to encapsulate what is truly and lastingly distinctive about his work. But "that damn word", as Pinter has dubbed it,[3] can sometimes be an apt description of the poet as his own poetaster.

There are, of course, certain commonplaces of Pinter criticism that can be passed over briefly not because they are wrong but because they are commonplaces—though it is surprising how many of these, rightly deduced from the work of Pinter's early years, continue to be insisted upon, with diminishing returns, in his later work. I claim no original insight, then, in declaring that in each of Pinter's earliest plays, *The Room*, *The Birthday Party* and *The Dumb Waiter*, the fourth wall of what some freudian punsters have called a living womb is opened out, revealing three more or less seedy apartments that at once nurture and threaten to betray their occupants. I have dubbed this sequence Pinter's "Domestic Interiors", for the hemming-in quality of each room is as integral to these plays as their human inhabitants—and, in the case of the one-act pieces, the room is almost as distinctively a "character" in the action.

It has been less often noticed that the second group of Pinter's plays moves as insistently outdoors as the first remained inside. Much less in dispute, though, is what these plays are *about*: and I hope that "Explanations and Definitions", the portmanteau-title I've given these less circumscribed works, suggests what *A Slight Ache* and *A Night Out*, together with the revue sketches Pinter contributed to *One to Another* and *Pieces of Eight*, have in common. For the sketches (of their kind as good as anything Pinter has written) are self-evidently "definitions"—dramatic vignettes which set their small-scale scenes in sparing verbal brushstrokes, and let them speak for themselves. And it is precisely the more "explanatory" nature of the two longer plays that flaws them. Human situations—marital in *A Slight Ache*, oedipal in *A Night Out*—are given definition. But for the single-frame, incisive caricature of the sketches is substituted a hogarthian progression of scenes which, lacking Hogarth's moral sense, moves towards a merely worked-up climax as dramatic truths are vitiated by theatrical twists.

The third group of plays rectifies this weakness—which, curiously (considering the alleged opacity of Pinter's writing), was essentially a fault of over-explication. Thus, the "Acceptances and Rejections" of *The Caretaker*, *Night School* and *The Dwarfs* explore more rigorously but less overtly the kind of human choices Pinter had utilised as psychological linking-devices in *A Slight Ache* and *A Night Out*. The apogee of his early career was reached during this period, in *The Caretaker*—and this achievement was not to be surpassed, in my view, till the writing of *Landscape* and *Silence* nearly a decade later.

Although the acts of acceptance and rejection are sometimes committed in a seemingly contradictory manner, their
inner logic is inextricably bound up with the processes by
which personal communication is rejected or thwarted, with
the evasions by which these processes are rationalised, and
with the ragged-edged rhetoric in which they are verbalised.
But the surreal development of *The Dwarfs* disguises its actual
similarity to *The Caretaker*. Both are plays in which characters
are deployed one against another, and Len in *The Dwarfs*
rejects the uncertainties of real friendships in favour of the
dwarfs of his own creation no less finally than Davies in *The
Caretaker* is edged-out of the relationship he has tried to
reshape to his own advantage. *Night School* holds up a mirror
image to these acts of exclusion: here, the outsider calls the
tune, and the departing stranger does the rejecting instead of
being rejected.

Of course, none of my attempted groupings is mutually
exclusive. *A Night Out*, as its title implies, is about an attempt
to escape from a living womb, just as *A Silent Ache* ends with
a definite—an over-definite—act of rejection. Similarly,
Night School anticipates Pinter's preoccupation with a theme
that was to dominate his next three plays. These—*The
Collection*, *The Lover* and *The Homecoming*—I have lumped
together as "The Love Chases": and they seem to me at
once the most explicit and the least satisfying works he has
written. Here, the feeling that Pinter had temporarily fallen
victim to his own influence is at its most cloying: he was, as it
were, wallowing in his dramatic individuality instead of
purifying and developing its promise.

Yet just as Pinter seemingly assimilated the lessons of *A
Slight Ache* and *A Night Out* in the plays which immediately
followed them, so his more recent work has been distinguished precisely by a formal discipline which *The Home-*

coming—for all its apparent paring-down to essentials—in particular lacked. Into this fifth and (so far as this book is concerned) final group I have gathered *Tea Party*, *The Basement*, *Landscape*, *Night*, *Silence* and *Old Times*—the very titles of those last four works hinting at an astringency which would be almost beckettian if Pinter had not become so much more precise in suggesting physical *locales* for his actions, utterly unlike the mounds, urns and benches of Beckett's later plays—as they are also unlike Pinter's earlier works. This group explores a succession of "Passing Acquaintances", and I have christened it accordingly: for in each of these six plays, human flotsam seems to touch and drift apart, causing a ripple—perhaps an illusory ripple—of contact, soon to be caught up and dispersed in the diverging currents of time.

None of Pinter's plays could be by anybody else, though a lot of other people's plays could pardonably be mistaken for jottings Pinter might have dispatched in the direction of his wastepaper basket. In itself, this distinctiveness is not all that hard to define. Neither is, say, the difference between *The Room*—in which the visual trappings are solid yet symbolic, and human needs can be compressed within four walls[4]—and *Landscape*, in which the physical location is precise yet boundless, and human existence is a matter of tenuous, half-remembered contacts with one's fellows. It is because it is so much more difficult to trace the changes of style, setting and mood *from one play to the next* that I have gone label-hunting, and come up with a few phrases intended to open out those successive, shifting levels of interest which it's tempting to bury beneath the convenient, superficial similarities of the merely "pinteresque".

As I have suggested in this introduction, which also amounts to the "argument" underlying the chapters which

follow, Pinter has himself seemed preoccupied more than
once with what is simply modish in his works—*A Slight Ache*
and *The Homecoming* seeming to me the most obvious examples
of his more inbred authorship. But in his major works—
—notably in *The Caretaker*, and in the imagist plays and
sketches of his early and later career—he has transcended the
more constricting features of his own style no less than the
limitations of my labels. One of my concerns in the pages
that follow has thus been to suggest a few critical conclusions
about each play and group of plays in a manner that will
illuminate Pinter's *development* as a dramatist, rather than
those aspects of his work which have remained constant—
and to investigate why those "constants" can contribute in
one case to making a play tedious and predictable, and in
another to the shaping of a masterpiece.

In the earlier studies in this series, a penultimate chapter
has discussed the personal, critical, political and other non-
dramatic writings of the playwright concerned. But Pinter is
among the most anonymous of writers, and not often forthcoming about his own work:[5] and when he *is* forthcoming,
he tends to commit one of the most dangerous of critical
fallacies, describing his characters either as extensions of
himself or as creations who have taken on some totally
independent existence, which is outside his artistic control.[6]
Unfortunately, no other members of his audiences happen to
be Harold Pinter. His own peculiar relationship with a work
of art may be inescapable for an author, but is irrelevant to
an audience—whose members must be at that further distance
from the original creative impulse than the readers of a poem
or a novel that is imposed by the overlay of the director's and
actors' interpretations, however sensitive these might be.

And so, while the interested reader will find Pinter's
occasional pronouncements listed in the Bibliography which

concludes this volume—along with the proliferating pronouncements of others about his work—it did not seem useful
to try to extrapolate from these scattered fragments such a
clearly formed attitude towards his plays and their purpose
as it is possible to find in the non-dramatic prose of an
Arnold Wesker, a John Whiting, or even a John Osborne.
Similarly, the brief Chronology of Pinter's life which is
among the other appendices to this volume deliberately
omits such tantalising glimpses of the origins of the plays in
incidents from life as are to be found in the much fuller
chronology in Martin Esslin's *The Peopled Wound* (to which,
factually, I gratefully acknowledge a debt).[7] For it seems to
me that if we are to appreciate Pinter's plays as the major
contributions to contemporary theatre I believe many of
them to be, they must be understood as independent works
of art—independent of their own accidental or even trivial
inspiration, and from what may or may not have been their
author's intentions—and accepted as the rich raw material
for performance upon a stage that, for directors and actors,
they demonstrably are.

It is because any such stage performance will, quite
properly, take on the colouring of its time and place, and be
shaped by the prejudices of those involved, that I have not
in the present work referred to specific performances of
Pinter's plays—though I have seen and reviewed most of
them in their original productions or major revivals. Here,
rather, I offer my own interpretive commentary. Occasionally, the emphasis is corrective, as in my attempts to demon-
strate the social and even political importance of some of the
plays, which may help to counterbalance the more common
tendency to psychologise Pinter almost out of existence—
whereas, in an earlier volume, it was helpful to insist on the
psychological interest of those plays of Osborne's which had

more usually been regarded as statements of social protest. But always the intention is that my understanding of the plays should spark usefully against the director's or the reader's contrasting ideas of their potential. It is in the hope of encouraging just such an active response from the reader, his own set of Pinter's plays to hand, that quotations from the texts are keyed to the page numbers of the individual editions published by Methuen, as cited in the Bibliography. For of all living playwrights Pinter surely stands most in need of rescue from the ivory-towered seeker after literary schools, or the doctorate-mongering writer of dissertations and image-gathering articles. It is in the belief that his plays *can* be brought acceptably and fruitfully down to earth, even if that earth is occasionally subject to erratic laws of gravity, that I offer the present study. It is intended to be suggestive rather than definitive, rooted in the words of the text and the possible ways of speaking them upon a stage rather than in extraneous philosophising: and, ultimately, it is as much a product of my own times as the plays are of Pinter's.

THE PLAYS OF HAROLD PINTER

Domestic Interiors

The Room, The Birthday Party and *The Dumb Waiter*

HAROLD PINTER wrote his first three plays, *The Room, The Birthday Party* and *The Dumb Waiter*, in quick succession during 1957. Thus, their similarity may be as much due to a current personal mood as to a common theme: certainly, each achieved a kind of self-sufficiency such as Pinter was never entirely able—or maybe did not wish—to recapture until his most recent work. Because of this, it's unwise to start peeling off layer after layer of "significance" so as to crack some inner kernel of dramatic truth: for a lingering odour of gyntian onions tends to be the only reward of over-exegesis. One demolishes at one's peril the physical, bricks-and-mortar settings which the plays share—for these have an indisputable solidity on the stage of a theatre, but only an arguable symbolism in the pages of a playbook. Anyway, nobody needs telling any longer that each play takes place within a four-walled setting, and that this setting serves a strongly protective purpose—although in each case the shelter of a room proves ultimately inadequate as a refuge from the threatening world outside.[8] All these generalisations can be justified, but they have become commonplaces of criticism: there is much besides at once to isolate and to universalise in Pinter's earliest plays.

Consider a few random ways of throwing light on the

three works. Think of them, for example, as dramatic versions of imagist poems—completed statements, at once terse and evocative. For one does perhaps need to know the plays *in their entirety* before one can sense the complexity of their strictly chronological movement: and this could be why *The Birthday Party*, so baffling and infuriating in its first production, became crystal clear to the baffled and infuriated when they read the play or saw it revived—now knowing exactly what was going to happen.[9]

Alternatively, look for mythic points of reference, and so regard the plays as modern reworkings of archetypal sexual situations—for which the Greeks had plenty of words, and for which the psychoanalysts have found plenty of meanings. *The Birthday Party* thus becomes a bourgeois re-enactment of an oedipal tragedy, whilst *The Room* inverts the related Antigone legend as a daughter refuses to accompany a blinded father into the unknown. *The Dumb Waiter*, in this light, is itself a Delphic Oracle gone to seed, delivering meaningless menus and finally demanding a human sacrifice.

Or, at the other extreme, take a cue from this last play's punning title and "interpret" it as a black revue-sketch—an elaborate exercise in crossed purposes with a twist in its tail—and reduce *The Room* to a modern melodrama. After all, Pinter himself has an even more mundane explanation for *The Birthday Party*: it is a play about a boarding-house he once stayed stayed in at the seaside, which had an over-powering, scraggy landlady and a screwed-up fellow-lodger.[10] All three plays, one might say, can be diluted—or concentrated—to taste.

However far-fetched—or over-simplified—some of the foregoing interpretations sound, the general point of the exercise is to suggest that the plays are better understood by analogy than by analysis, and that within certain individual limits, *any* analogy will serve. Their essence precedes their existence: and they are more than merely symbolic *because* their existentialism is thus inverted. The transcendence of action over character shapes men and women into traditional moulds, so that the spectator gives himself up not only to a traditional conflict of forces, but to a strangely familiar pattern of events. And there are two theatrical forms— meeting as the spectrum of dramatic genres turns full circle— in which events tend to shape instead of being shaped by characters. These forms are tragedy and farce.

The label invented by Martin Esslin to describe their convergence[11] is, of course, theatre of the absurd: but here such a term would introduce, I think, a needless hint of innovation into a long-acknowledged kind of affinity. Aristotle, after all, didn't rate characterisation as an especially important tragic quality. Certainly, he subordinated it to the necessity for unity of action: and it is precisely this unity—a classicised way of describing self-containment— which makes Pinter's earliest three plays so strikingly traditional, however superficially surprising the means by which characters allow themselves to be manipulated to its requirements.

One other unity observed by Pinter in these three plays— though it is more augustan than aristotelian—is, of course, unity of place. It is its single setting which first pins down each action—yet which permits everyman in an audience his own associations. In the preciseness of the physical location is its metaphysical freedom. In this respect, it is even notable that each successive play descends one storey lower in what could well be—atmospherically though not architecturally—a single house. *The Room* itself—apparently what the shop-window postcards call a bed-sit with cooking facilities—is on some unspecified upper floor of which the landlord (if landlord he be) has long ago lost count. [102] *The Birthday Party* is held in the dining-room-cum-lounge of Meg's boarding house. And *The Dumb Waiter* descends into just such a dark, damp basement as that in which Riley waited to visit Rose Hudd in *The Room*.

That a shared street-number would make geographical nonsense doesn't much matter. Meg, proud though she is of being "on the list", [17] has more paying-guests in her mind than her visitor's book; the dumb waiter relays orders from non-existent customers in a non-existent restaurant up-stairs; and Rose Hudd has no idea what goes on outside the front-door of her flat. Each "room" is part of a confidence-trick in which the victim is voluntarily taking part—voluntarily, because one must be aware of one's free-will before one can abdicate it. Each room could as well be a "real" place in which a self-induced deception has dulled reality, or an encapsulated ritual in some seedy, provincial version of Genet's *Balcony*. Thus does an Englishman's home become Kafka's *Castle*.

The action of *The Room* takes place on a cold winter's evening, that of *The Birthday Party* begins on a bright summer's morning, and that of *The Dumb Waiter* occurs at dead of night. And so on: the temptation to seek some system or significance which will tidy the plays into a trilogy is strong—but, in the end, it has to be resisted. It's not important that Rose Hudd's room is apparently in London, Meg's boarding house on the South coast, and Ben and Gus's basement in Birmingham: one can't even be sure that they are, for nothing outside the three rooms is proven or required to be proven, and their postal addresses could, for all they matter, have remained as doubtful as the real Christian names of Rose Hudd and Goldberg. What does

matter is that one should first recognise the self-containment
the dramatist has imposed on his plays, and then take one's
own flights of fancy from there.

Critics often drift into an alluringly ambiguous musical
terminology in talking about Pinter: so, to follow suit, it may
be helpful to think of these three works not as successive
movements in some great symphonic whole, but as self-
sufficient variations on familiar themes—familiar both
superficially, according to any or all of the analogies already
suggested, and also in the underlying, almost classical sense
of inevitability which they share. Irresistibly, then, one
returns to that feature which the plays have in common
with one another, as with those genres which are capable
of containing archetypal qualities without suffocating individuality: that is, the dramatic forms in which character
traditionally succumbs to action, and in which the unity
or self-containment of that action has traditional authority—
the forms of tragedy and farce.

In a period of generic disintegration, what has taken place
has not only been the breakdown of a set of conventions
which segmented tears and laughter into separate halves of
some ultimate double-bill, but also—and particularly to the
present point—a recognition that the antipodean gap between
farce and tragedy is created by the dramatist not the drama.
For in both forms, the fates mount a concerted attack on
a chosen sufferer: and it is only a difference in the playwright's point of view—a broken pair of braces in his sights
instead of a broken heart—that distinguishes the farceur's
description of domesticity from the tragedian's trail of destruction and death.

Both tragedy and farce, in short, are about humanity *in
extremis*. "Regular" comedy is not: it throws into relief either
the normalities or the eccentricities of everyday life, and it

tends towards either the mannered (after the restoration model) or the humorous (in the jonsonian vein) accordingly. So the description "comedy of menace", which even Pinter himself (not usually a man for labels) has considered appropriate to his first three or four plays,[12] is not strictly valid—except, perhaps, to *A Slight Ache*. Menace there is, sure enough; but *comedy* cannot be so cut off, so devoid of social context, as are the people and places of these first three plays. But farce, like tragedy, does close its circle upon its heroes-turned-victims—upon, in short, the biters bit. In each of Pinter's earliest plays, the bites prove fatal—which makes them, if anything, tragi-farces.

But what's in a name, anyway? Why fuss about generic traditions when it is precisely the originality of the plays in question that excites? Because, surely, a generic approach to any kind of play should suggest . . . no, not how to pinion it into a critic's straitjacket, but how to discover what it is *not* setting out to do—and how, therefore, to avoid criticising the omission of what, within certain formal boundaries, shouldn't be expected to be there anyway. Some boundaries are made to be crossed: but they can also exert a valuable dramatic discipline. They hem in Pinter's earliest plays both physically and formally, and in so doing give them shape and definition—whereas if those plays had been "true" comedies, one would no doubt have found similar limitations arbitrarily restrictive.

In turning to the earliest of them all, *The Room*, first staged at Bristol University in 1957, and professionally in a double-bill with *The Dumb Waiter* in 1960, let's conversely consider first the character who has most generally been condemned—for ignoring restrictions which, in fact, the play's form *never* imposes. That character is the blind Negro in the basement called Riley. And his function in *The Room* is crucial because on it the success or failure of the much-maligned climax depends.

Rose Hudd gives her husband Bert his tea, talks at him (getting no word of reply), and is visited by Kidd—apparently the landlord, though he doesn't seem to know or remember much about his own property. The menfolk depart, and Rose, taking out the day's rubbish, is confronted on her doorstep by a younger couple, Mr and Mrs Sands, who have been told by a mysterious stranger in the dark of the basement that the Hudds' own room is to let. The couple are looking for the landlord, but are convinced that his name is not Kidd. On their departure Kidd shuttles back in, anxious that Mrs Hudd should see the stranger in the basement, who has been pestering him all weekend to arrange a meeting. Reluctantly agreeing, Rose claims not to recognise Riley—but he begs her to "come home", [118] and is struck brutally to the floor by the returning, momentarily articulate Bert. As Riley collapses, Rose finds that she herself is blind; and the play ends, appropriately, with a blackout.

The room itself is replete with the common-or-kitchen props on which Pinter so often depends—a gas-fire, sink, stove, rocking-chair. At once snug, stuffy and a bit down-at-heel. A double-bed protruding from an alcove, completes the self-containment of the place. An audience's expectation might be of a problem play—its problem no doubt a petty one—serio-comic and perhaps condescending in tone.

As in *The Birthday Party*, a poor thing of a meal opens the proceedings—Bert Hudd's supper, as opposed to Stanley's breakfast—and its desultory, one-sided verbal accompaniment contrasts the cold weather outside with the warmth and security within, and the home comforts of the Hudds' bed-sit with the damp and darkness of the basement. These three "givens" of the situation—the room, the basement, the outside—are merged into one of Rose's longest unbroken speech-segments just before Mr Kidd makes his entrance:

> This is a good room. You've got a chance in a place like this. I look after you, don't I, Bert? Like when they offered us the basement here I said no straight off. I knew that'd be no good. The ceiling right on top of you. No, you've got a window here, you can move yourself, you can come home at night, if you have to go out, you can do your job, you can come home, you're all right. And I'm here. You stand a chance. [99]

And the play is really "about" the threatening and finally the destruction of this status quo.

Yet one does sense the need to hedge that last statement with its inverted commas. It implies development, whereas the action is more of a completed statement: its end is implicit in its beginning. All the talk and the cosy cups of tea are hopeless gestures of defiance against a brooding nemesis. In Boris Vian's *Empire Builders*, that bundle of not-quite-humanity called the Schmürz pursues a family from floor to floor of *their* tenement block: and in *The Room* the same kind of semi-reality is omnipresent, awaiting its opportunity to crawl up from the basement. The Matchseller of *A Slight Ache* was actually to assume a physical resemblance to the Schmürz—the nameless horror in the censored but sub-consciously remembered freudian nightmare, embodying both a trauma from the past and a premonition of the future. In short, and in the formalised terms of tragedy, he personi-fies retribution. And in *The Room* he happens to take the form of the blind Negro.

How dare he be so obtrusively symbolic? Yet in the physical sense, at least, the Negro is quite flagrantly nonsymbolic. He is both black and blind—racially and physically different, yet daring to invoke the racial kinship of father-hood, and inflicting the bodily deformity of blindness. Now Pinter's own cultural inheritance of Jewishness, unlike Wesker's, can be sensed in the subtext rather than the subject-matter of his plays, so that here an assimilated sense of persecution erupts in a seedy suburban microcosm. A culture is compounded of its own values and of the values imposed upon it, so that persecutors and persecuted alike participate in a sort of secularised liturgy. Rose Hudd is recalled to her race—indeed, to her family, for the Negro's demands are patriarchal. Bert Hudd strikes down the enfeebled old man, but it is Rose who suffers the conse-quences of his violence. Husband and father engage in a mythic struggle for possession of the female, the object of whose suppressed fears and desires finally confronts her. . . .

The Negro, then, is both more and less than symbolic. He *is* a Negro, current focus for racist abuse at its most irration-ally virulent (significantly, the one word of attention Bert Hudd pays him is to call him a lice). [120] And in so far as he might once have been a Catholic, an American Indian or a Jew he is . . . no, not so much symbolic as representative. He might even have been, as his name implies, an Irishman—the One Eyed Riley, perhaps of the song, now quite blind, who had been the Unidentified Guest in Eliot's *Cocktail Party* besides. But according to Eliot's anglo-catholic tenets, Riley is a means of redemption: according to Pinter's judaic tradition, he is the "slight ache" in Mrs Hudd's life who threatens retribution.

Not—or so Rose Hudd enigmatically claims—that Riley is the real name of her unidentified guest. [118] And other doubts about the names of characters—Riley addresses Rose as Sal, [118–19] and Mr Sands is certain that he didn't speak

B

to anybody called Kidd [105]—contribute to an ambiguity, a sense of not getting to grips with things or with people, that permeates the whole play. Kidd, pestered by Rose with the polite questions of small-talk, scarcely ever gives a direct answer. And both he [104] and Mr Sands [108] cast oblique doubt on Bert Hudd's safety outside—though Bert's skill as a driver is interminably reiterated by his wife, no doubt to increase her own confidence in it. Trivial things take on sudden importance: whether or not Mrs Sands saw a star on her way, [107–8] whether Mr Sands was sitting down or perching [110]—tiny semantic quibbles, like Ben and Gus's argument about lighting the gas in *The Dumb Waiter*. [135–6] Amplifications, usually needless, tend to obscure the simplest statements. And the disquieting effect of the successive visitors is cumulative.

Kidd is apparently no more than evasive, though he's given to vaguely disturbing little remarks like his revelation that the Hudds' room was once his own. [101] But the presence of the Sands is more ominous, quite explicitly posing a threat to the Hudds' own tenancy. [112] And, whilst Kidd is demonstrably from the same world—the same house—as the Hudds (in his clipped beckettian name as in his style), the Sands seem to have wandered in from a different sort of play. Christian-named Toddy and Clarissa, they keep crossing their own rather middle-class purposes: indeed, the only things they agree on are those which throw doubt on Mrs Hudd's own domestic assumptions. And the third visitor, the most complete outsider of all, finally shatters not only Mrs Hudd's assurance but her identity as well.

It's interesting to note how Mrs Hudd herself swops assumptions to taste when fending off Riley's presence. At one moment he is an "old, poor blind man," one of "these creeps" who "come in, smelling up my room". But just a few sentences later, the Negro is accused of attacking the land-lord, and it is Kidd who becomes the "poor, weak old man". [117] Apart from fitting into the patterned ambivalence of the play, this also, and significantly, echoes just the kind of double-talk with which the prejudiced try to rationalise their racialism in real life: coloured people, for example, are, as best befits the argument, said to be degenerate, yet threaten-ingly powerful; disease-infested yet potent; indistinguishable in appearance yet a seductive threat to the nations' white womanhood. "You're all deaf and dumb and blind, the lot of you," screams Mrs Hudd. "A bunch of cripples." [117] But, retributively, when Bert Hudd suddenly finds his voice in his moment of violence, it is an unfinished reference by the Negro to his wife that stirs him into his final spasm of aroused sexual jealousy. And it is Rose who suffers vicariously and becomes one of the "cripples" she despises. [120]

One wonders whether critics would have responded quite so obtusely towards the character of the blind Negro if Pinter had written *The Room* ten years later. That it antici-pated England's own increased racial tensions was not in itself either prophetic or remarkable, however—for the *attitudes* it dramatises repeat themselves in most forms of racialism, anti-semitism included. Nor, of course, is it sufficient simply to say: this play is an allegory about the colour problem, which shows how we fashion the unfamiliar according to our own image until it either overwhelms us, as it does Rose, or enables us to find a perverted outlet for such pent-up energies as Bert's, by opposing it with violence. But if we allow the possibility that this is *one* of the things *The Room* is about, not only is its self-containment no longer flawed by the character of the blind Negro, but its elements of "absurdism" become more than vaguely menacing portents.[13]

Their menace, indeed, becomes double-edged; Rose Hudd has reason to be afraid *because* she is afraid, and her fear manifests itself in a pre-emptive hostility. A passive desire for security becomes an active agent of evil, and all the ambiguity and evasive dialogue becomes not an amusing stylistic mannerism but an effect—and in its turn a cause—of the fear of the dark outside. And the room of the title—though it *does* symbolise security, the womb, and what have you—is also quite simply a room which is *not* to let. One of the loopholes in the Race Relations Act, it's not irrelevant to note, preserved the Englishman's right to refuse a coloured lodger, but no longer to advertise his prejudice on his shop-window postcard.

I think this approach helps to meet some of the objections to the "overtly symbolic" nature of the blind Negro—the objection to the very immediacy of his presence as "a parody of a Prévert embodiment of fate", for instance.[14] Such an objection is surely mistaken not only on the particular ground that he doesn't embody blind fate at all, simply a blind Negro, but on the more general ground that it presupposes both a lack of reason in Rose's fears and an audience's automatic sympathy for them. For is not Rose in fact the biter bit, the victim of a tragical-farcical nemesis which her own fallibility has set in motion? As such, she is indeed a pitiable person, but she is also a guilty one—guilty both of apathy and of ignorance.

The Birthday Party, on which Pinter started work immediately after seeing the first production of *The Room*, was staged, briefly and disastrously, in London in May 1958—though the production had been relatively well-received on tour by Oxford and Cambridge audiences. Like *The Room*, this play is also about guilt, but here the theme is much more elaborately predicated by the action. On the surface, this is—or rather, is what was soon to be dubbed—conventional comedy of menace. Two strangers, Goldberg and McCann, arrive in a scruffy seaside boarding-house run by the inanely sentimental Meg—who treats Stanley, her only other lodger, more like a spoilt, overgrown child than a paying guest. In spite of his apparent detestation of Meg's mothering, and his awed shrinking from the sexual advances of Lulu, the girl-next-door, Stanley's dependence both upon the place and Meg's person is evidently strong. The arrival of the strangers, however, marks the beginning of a planned persecution of Stanley—to which Meg and Lulu become unwitting accomplices during the grotesque "birthday party" of the title, given for Stanley in the middle act. By the next morning and the third act, he has been rendered both speechless and helpless: and, in spite of a token opposition put up by Meg's usually docile, deck-chair attendant of a husband, Petey, he is taken unresisting away.

The Birthday Party is many plays to many men. It has been said to be "about" the irresistible pressures of conformity, presumably because Stanley, normally scruffy, appears bowler-hatted and besuited in the last act. More convincingly, it can be conceived as an oedipal tragi-farce set in a seaside lodging house. And it is, allegorically, a working-out of revenge and an expiation of guilt, in which two exploited and spat-upon races turn the tables upon their persecutor, terrorising him out of his funk-hole: for Goldberg and McCann are, after all, the other two victims in the twentieth century's unfunny story about the Negro, the Jew and the Irishman. "To me," says Stanley—Pinter's second biter to be turned on by the bitten—"you're nothing but a dirty joke. I have responsibilities towards the people in this house. . . . They've lost their sense of smell." [48] The aggression is impotent, but its idiom is familiar.

Of course, the action here is much more complex than that of *The Room*, but its main conflict *can* be identified as the gradual wearing-away of Stanley's resistance to the covert but threatening advances of his two mysterious fellow-lodgers: this, however, is complicated not by other outsiders, like Mr Kidd and the Sands (who merely kept an action moving towards its climax), but by Stanley's fellow "insiders"—his landlady, her husband, and the available Lulu. The reactions of these characters—or their refusals to react—become just as important as Stanley's own progress towards oblivion: indeed, they become all-important in the last act, during which Stanley himself utters nothing more than a few inarticulate gurgles.[15]

The canvas of the play, like that of *The Room*, is best assimilated as a whole, before being studied more closely, tapestry-wise, in its sequential parts: but the design is now much more complex. Many threads which have since become familiar in the new drama can be separated-out from it—the landlady–lodger relationship, for example, which is to be found in Osborne and Creighton's naturalistic *Epitaph for George Dillon*, in the heightened social realism of Edward Bond's *Saved*, or in Orton's farcical-lyrical *Entertaining Mr Sloane*; and what in Osborne's work had been a textbook case of subverted mother-love becomes here, as in the plays of Bond and Orton, frankly sexual and so oedipal.

When the play begins, it's not until Stanley is well into his breakfast that there's any indication that he is not Meg and Petey's son, but their lodger—and Meg evidently doesn't think of him in these terms, as the eventual, casual revelation of their real relationship suggests:

STANLEY: Visitors? Do you know how many visitors you've had since I've been here?

MEG: How many?
STANLEY: One.
MEG: Who?
STANLEY: Me! I'm your visitor. [17]

At this moment, all the earlier banter between Meg and Petey shifts into a new gear—and the tendency the audience will have noticed for any subject to gravitate towards Stanley is thus seen to be not a sign of parental fussiness, but a sexual byplay. Even the society gossip in the paper, from which Petey dredges up the gobbet of news that "somebody's just had a baby", has to be seen in a new light:

MEG: What is it?
PETEY [*studying the paper*]: Er—a girl.
MEG: Not a boy?
PETEY: No.
MEG: Oh, what a shame. I'd be sorry. I'd much rather have a little boy.
PETEY: A little girl's all right.
MEG: I'd much rather have a little boy. [11]

One's retrospective reaction to this passage emphasises what I mean by the necessity of digesting the play whole before ruminating over its parts: the simultaneous awareness that Stanley is *not* Meg's "little boy", but that she and Petey are discussing him as if he were, is much more helpful than the jolt from one state of awareness to the other inevitable on first acquaintance with the play. Later, Meg will be at one moment scolding Stanley like a naughty schoolboy, at the next ruffling his hair, or, "sensual, stroking his arm"— gestures which cause Stanley to recoil in disgust, and which emphasise the quasi-incestuous nature of the landlady-lodger relationship. [18–20]

Stanley, then, is over-mothered, and, maybe in consequence, both sexually and personally inadequate. He fails to
respond to the blatant but good-natured come-hithering of
Lulu, who sums him up as "a bit of a wash-out", [28] and in
his attraction–repulsion towards the two strangers a sublimated homosexuality might make psychological sense in
production, although it's not elaborated in the script. Or is
all such emotional extrapolation a mistaking of symbol for
substance? Well, it does provide a frame-of-reference for the
play, which fits it surprisingly snugly, and which, in tying up
what is otherwise a loose-end, merges two of its more important themes—those of sexual impotence and of racial antagonism. Without the psychologising, there is little point in
Stanley's attempt successively to strangle Meg and to
assault Lulu as his birthday party nears its climax. But
neither the rebellion against the mother-figure nor the rape
which might assert his freedom and prove his potency is
successful. Picked out by the torch-spotlight in the darkness,
Stanley capitulates, flattening himself against the wall,
giggling, as Goldberg and McCann converge upon him.
[66–8] And by the next morning, Goldberg has seduced Lulu
effortlessly, and Stanley has been rendered finally impotent.

The reversal of the racial stereotyping—the Aryan
prisoner cowering in the concentration-camp spotlight, his
Jewish warder ravishing the other's intended sexual partner
—is almost too obvious to need explicating. And Pinter
doesn't spell it out as it's happening—but he does anticipate
it, in that brief, stark indictment of Stanley which comes
between his nonsense-catechising at the hands of Goldberg
and McCann and the birthday party proper:

MCCANN: Wake him up. Stick a needle in his eye.
GOLDBERG: You're a plague, Webber. You're an overthrow.

MCCANN: You're what's left.

GOLDBERG: But we've got the answer to you. We can sterilise you.

MCCANN: What about Drogheda?

GOLDBERG: Your bite is dead. Only your pong is left.

MCCANN: You betray our land.

GOLDBERG: You betray our breed.

MCCANN: Who are you, Webber?

GOLDBERG: What makes you think you exist?

MCCANN: You're dead.

GOLDBERG: You're dead. You can't live, you can't think, you can't love. You're dead. You're a plague gone bad. There's no juice in you. You're nothing but an odour. [55]

After this, to talk about the play as if it were *merely* about a weak character overwhelmed by the forces of conformity[16] is surely not so much to over-simplify as to mislead. It's far truer to say that here the existential horror of existence is being probed until identity itself is effaced: yet this is to put the effect before the cause. For the cause, according to McCann the Irishman is nationalistic betrayal, whilst according to Goldberg the Jew it is racial impurity. The "dirty joke" has been turned against Stanley with a vengeance—and vengeance is its point.

I don't want to analyse the two most *verbally* compelling passages in the play—the interrogation of Stanley by Goldberg and McCann in act two, [50–5] and their "wooing" of him in act three [86–8]—too closely. Their similarity to the terrorising of A. G. in Whiting's *Conditions of Agreement* has already been noted,[17] and they do, quite literally, speak for themselves—the use of non-sequiturs, of household names, of a logic rooted in the pun and the least consequential connective, reaching a new pitch of terror. But it's worth recalling Pinter's own description of how he warded off with just such a random word-flow the recurrent threats from the petty fascists of his East End boyhood:

> If you looked remotely like a Jew you might be in trouble. Also, I went to a Jewish club, by an old railway arch, and there were quite a lot of people often waiting with broken bottles—*we* didn't have any milk bottles. The best way was to talk to them, you know, sort of, "Are you all right?" "Yes, I'm all right." "Well, that's all right then, isn't it?" And all the time keep walking towards the lights of the main road.[18]

Goldberg and McCann have no broken milk bottles either: their armoury is of words—and in this case their weapons are not defensive but offensive, battering down Stanley's feeble resistance until he stutters into speechlessness.

Meg is more Stanley's weight for verbal bullying—and in this passage, at the beginning of the play, the irony of his threats lies both in his own feeble employment of the tactics which are to be turned so effectively against him, and, of course, in the prophetic nature of his threat that "They're coming today."

MEG: Who?
STANLEY: They're coming in a van.
MEG: Who?
STANLEY: And do you know what they've got in that van?
MEG: What?
STANLEY: They've got a wheelbarrow in that van.
MEG [*breathlessly*]: They haven't.
STANLEY: Oh yes they have.
MEG: You're a liar.

STANLEY [*advancing upon her*]: A big wheelbarrow. And when the van stops they wheel it out, and they wheel it up the garden path, and then they knock at the front door.
MEG. They don't.
STANLEY: They're looking for someone.
MEG: They're not.
STANLEY: They're looking for someone. A certain person.
MEG [*hoarsely*]: No, they're not.
STANLEY: Shall I tell you who they're looking for?
MEG: No!
STANLEY: You don't want me to tell you?
MEG: You're a liar. [24–5]

They are, indeed, "coming today". They are, indeed, "looking for someone". But Meg, very relieved that the big car which turns up next morning doesn't contain a wheelbarrow, fails to recognise them. [71–2]

Where, this prompts the question, does Meg come into it at all? Or Lulu? Or Petey? Why is the location of the play in a seaside boarding-house so important? In an interview, Pinter himself has explained the genesis of *The Birthday Party* as follows:

It was sparked off from a very distinct situation in digs when I was on tour. In fact the other day a friend of mine gave me a letter I wrote him in nineteen-fifty something, Christ knows when it was. This is what it says, "I have filthy insane digs, a great bulging scrag of a woman with breasts rolling at her belly, an obscene household, cats, dogs, filth, tea-strainers, mess, oh bullocks, talk, chat rubbish shit scratch dung poison, infantility, deficient order in the upper fretwork, fucking roll on. . . ." Now the thing about this is *that* was *The Birthday Party*—I was in those digs and this woman was Meg in the play, and there was a fellow staying there in Eastbourne, on the coast.[19]

Asked later in the same interview, whether "the picture of a personal threat which is sometimes presented in your plays is troubling in a larger sense, a political sense", Pinter declared himself more or less uninterested in the structure of politics, but went on:

I'll tell you what I really think about politicians. The other night I watched some politicians on television talking about Vietnam. I wanted very much to burst through the screen with a flame-thrower and burn their eyes out and their balls off and then enquire from them how they would assess this action from a political point of view.[20]

To me *The Birthday Party* is a startling fusion of the impulses revealed in these two quotations: the one creative, the transposition into theatrical terms of a peculiarly vivid yet oppressive personal experience, and the other destructive— but destructive in a manner born of frustration with the futility of canting party-political chat about a safely-distant war. In this sense *The Birthday Party* is closer perhaps to Max Frisch's *The Fire Raisers* than to any contemporary British play—for it, too, is a domestication of apathy in the face of violence, of the turning not of the other cheek towards pain inflicted upon oneself, but of the blind eye towards humiliation inflicted on others.

Thus, at an allegorical level, Goldberg and McCann can be seen as the instruments of a racial vengeance: but at the level of the actual, they are precisely what they appear to be —brutal though not unsubtle persecutors of a hapless victim. At both levels, not one of the witnesses of the persecution does a thing to stop it. Lulu offers herself as a sexual sop to Goldberg's appetite. Meg is too obtusely dumb to register what is really happening. And only Petey, in the last act, offers any sort of resistance to the abduction of his lodger. His role in the action is, at first sight, reminiscent of Bert Hudd's in *The Room*: he has a little more to say for himself, but over breakfast he is as much the straight-man to a dramatically dominant wife as is Bert over his tea. Yet one already notices the tiny and surely deliberate differences.

Bert had a rasher for his tea, [96] but Meg, typically, has run out of bacon. [12] Rose Hudd pours out her husband's tea for him: but Petey, as Meg dawdles aimlessly, doesn't even have time for a cup. [16] Small points: but they are typical of the way in which Pinter establishes the human values and vacillations under the verbosity. However little he may say, Bert Hudd is boss in his own household—and it is thus dramatically, though not morally, right that in the end he should assert his supposed rights over his woman. But Petey is submerged beneath the "chat rubbish shit scratch dung poison" of his marriage, and at first one gives him up for lost. Yet in retrospect—and, again, how much more meaningful Petey's role in the first act does become in the light of his actions in the third—he achieves more independence of his environment than either Stanley or Meg.

He doesn't come to the birthday party—it's his "chess night", [47] a nice little character-touch of an explanation— and when he learns of Stanley's "nervous breakdown" the next morning he suggests sending for the doctor, and offers sellotape to mend his broken spectacles. [75–6] Dissuaded from both these common-sensical solutions by Goldberg, but reluctant to leave for the beach as he is urged, he goes into the garden "to see how my peas are getting on". [77] He returns just as Stanley is being taken out to the car, and he

makes a feeble but, in the circumstances, brave little effort to
save him. As the three move towards the door, he cries out
to them:

> PETEY: Leave him alone:
>   *They stop. Goldberg studies him.*
> GOLDBERG [*insidiously*]: Why don't you come with us, Mr
> Boles?
> MCCANN: Yes, why don't you come with us?
> GOLDBERG: Come with us to Monty. There's plenty of
> room in the car.
>   *Petey makes no move. They pass him and reach the door. McCann
>   opens the door and picks up the suitcases.*
> PETEY [*broken*]: Stan. don't let them tell you what to
> do: [90]

The gesture of defiance is a tiny one, but it is also the only
one anybody makes in the play. Petey has stood up to the
microcosmic fascist takeover one degree more forcefully,
though no less ineffectually, than Frisch's Herr Biedermann.

Pinter's allegory is at once simpler and more profound
than Frisch's, whose directly propagandist aim concentrated
the responsibility for fire-raising on the middle-classes—who
hope fire raisers will go away if they're nice to them, or pretend not to notice them. Frisch's dramatic situations and
relationships are all evolved to that end: but in *The Birthday
Party* there is going on simultaneously an allegory about the
rise of fascism, a seaside social comedy, and a sexual farce.
The play's focus is thus constantly shifting, so that the only
point-of-view which is never allowed to dominate the
action—allowing even Petey his moment of glory—is,
strangely, Stanley's.

Meg has no private parts: her character continually surfaces because it is so near to the surface. And Lulu hasn't much else but her private part, which she flaunts at the most attractive male in prospect. Yet Stanley himself is in many ways more enigmatic than either Goldberg or McCann. Reputedly a hack concert pianist, most of his "professional" reminiscences contradict themselves, and he is allowed none of the revelatory, off-duty moments of his persecutors. On the contrary, it's as if he were, indeed, under constant surveillance, and aware of it—like, aptly enough, a prisoner in a condemned cell.

Even Stanley's attempts at self-assertion are pale shadows of other people's: he is merely an object of other people's existences, whether of Meg's mothering or of Goldberg and McCann's more sinister paternalism. And yet, although he is the victim of a verbal beating-up, he is himself the only person to use *physical* violence in the play—kicking Goldberg in the stomach, [55] besides assaulting Meg and Lulu. [66–8] Maybe, to take the action on its own terms, he has really deserted "the organisation", as McCann accuses? [51] If so, we never hear the confession of his faults—"all that . . . talking"—which is made to McCann on the morning-after, before Stanley lapses finally into silence. [76] At last, dressed immaculately but for his broken glasses, he can emit nothing but gurgles and the snatched half-words of baby-talk.

In comparison, Goldberg and McCann acquire quite familiar, almost human shapes. There is something weirdly compulsive yet intently characteristic about McCann's habit of tearing newspapers into equal strips—indeed, it seems almost indelicate, a breach of good manners, for Goldberg to rebuke him for it. [78] And Goldberg's hypochondria, [80–3] like his otiose rhetoric which has a way of trailing off into absent-minded banality when he's not, as it were, on the job, is another humanising factor. What matters about the couple's casual exchanges and their demonstrations of their own fallibility is that these should modify one's sense of inevitability—and usefully so. The outcome of the action is a conflict—albeit an unequal one—not a foregone conclusion. The tragi-farce is euripidean, not—as, say, in Whiting's *Saint's Day*—aeschylian.[21] And this is why it's so important that, Stanley's resistance broken, Petey should stir himself into life.

Objectively, it is only when the action on stage is completed that it becomes inevitable—the play, once witnessed, becomes both immutable and *familiar*, so that it is its *substance* that matters on a second or subsequent visit, not the irrecoverable suspense of one's first acquaintance. To wonder overmuch what is going to happen, as an audience strange to the play must do, is to increase the likelihood of its failing: but to come to the play with foreknowledge of what is going to happen, yet at the same time to remain aware that it *needn't* have happened, is to open out the action, so that it truly becomes itself. Thus, it mirrors the regrets for the words unspoken, the sins of omission, in one's own past—the regrets, like the play, more tragic because all is now past remedying, yet also absurd and inconsequential because, but for a slip of the tongue or a fatal hesitancy, nothing need have happened at all. Stanley's abduction need not have happened at all. Hitler need not have happened at all. And it wasn't Stanley's birthday, anyway.

Or was it? The ambiguity is unresolved, but Pinter doesn't press it too hard. If he did, it might defeat its own ends, as does this verbalisation of Meg's shortage of lodgers:

STANLEY: Has Meg had many guests staying in this house, besides me, I mean before me?

LULU: Besides you?
STANLEY [*impatiently*]: Was she very busy, in the old days?
LULU: Why should she be?
STANLEY: What do you mean? This used to be a boarding house, didn't it?
LULU: Did it?
STANLEY: Didn't it?
LULU: Did it?
STANLEY: Didn't . . . oh, skip it. [28]

The exchange could all too well have been skipped, for it threatens to pin down the play according to a logic that is not its own, and it hints at the trap of self-parody which Pinter was to fall into for a period after his first burst of creative activity.

Ambiguous nomenclature, too, here becomes more of a mannerism than a means. Goldberg, normally Nat, calls himself both Simey [46] and Benny, [81] quickly double-taking himself out of the first slip, but getting furious when McCann uses the name too. It's McCann who also points out that Goldberg refers to his son both as Manny and Timmy during one of his rambling excursions into his family history—and Goldberg even accuses Stanley of having changed his name during the interrogation:

GOLDBERG: Webber! Why did you change your name?
STANLEY: I forgot the other one. [53]

Now the mistakes of nomenclature conform well enough to the nature of Goldberg's reminiscences, which at best have a random air about them, and to the form taken by the catechising of Stanley. The trouble is that one is beginning to recognise the trick as idiosyncratically Pinter's, rather than his characters'.

The use of place names, on the other hand, remains successful, because their poeticising in everyday speech is one of the real-life mannerisms Pinter was among the first to recognise and turn to dramatic purpose. The front-of-bus effect of Stanley's one and only concert having been given at Lower Edmonton is exactly right after his geography-book grabbing of romantic-sounding foreign names during the fantasising about a "round the world tour".[23] This, too, is a trick, but it is a trick to lead one into Stanley's mind, not into Pinter's.

The Birthday Party, like all the best of Pinter's early work, is the more terrifying because even its so-called ritualistic elements are really rather prosaic—in origin albeit not in action. And they are rooted in character rather than externalised: thus, the birthday gift of a toy drum for Stanley is a consummately skilful example of reality turned to ritualistic purpose. Meg has brought it for him because he hasn't got a piano, [38] and the gesture emerges from her combination of insensitivity and clumsy tenderness. Similarly, the frenzied drum-beating which closes the first act typifies Stanley's known tendency to let his inadequacy combine with his contempt to urge him into violent yet petty acts of cruelty or defiance. Here too, however, the gesture is prophetic—and certainly symbolic, for Stanley himself is now summoning his antagonists into action.

The use of the drum at the end of the second act at once sustains and gives shape to its dramatic function, as Stanley, the thing caught on his foot, limps along, a sexual, moral, and now a physical cripple. Yet in the light of the next morning the broken toy which Meg picks out of the fireplace becomes as pathetic, as grotesque, and also as *objectified* as its owner:

MEG: The drum's broken. [*Petey looks up.*] Why is it broken?

PETEY: I don't know.

She hits it with her hand.

MEG: It still makes a noise.

PETEY: You can always get another one.

MEG [*sadly*]: It was probably broken in the party. I don't remember it being broken though, in the party. [70]

The exact but unstated parallel here between the shattered instrument and its crippled owner may not even be intentional: it is *there* nevertheless, signifying the assurance, conscious or unconscious, with which Pinter in *The Birthday Party* has rendered his metaphysical material in terms of his physical minutiae. And it is of the essence that this raw material should be of the most commonplace and trivial kind—an objective correlative which gives universality and intensity to the play's subject, and terror to its subtext.

The Dumb Waiter, the last of the three plays Pinter wrote during 1957, had to wait another three years for its first performance, in a double-bill with *The Room*. The service-lift of this one-acter's title is a sort of *machina ex deis*, which operates to and from a basement that was once—perhaps still is—the kitchen of a cafe. Here, Ben and Gus, the play's only characters, are awaiting instructions from the boss of some vague but evidently well-organised underworld gang. And so Pinter's storey-by-storey exploration finally descends from that upper-floor *Room*, by way of the ground-floor lounge of *The Birthday Party*, into the windowless and no doubt damp basement so feared by Rose Hudd.

Goldberg and McCann were reduced to homelier proportions in *The Birthday Party* when caught off the job, and thus off their guard—indeed, the very reference to the terrorising of Stanley Webber as "a job" [31] added its touch of reality. Ben and Gus might almost be instruments of the same anonymous "organisation" as Goldberg and McCann—but, less bright and ready-tongued, and therefore a few rungs down the salary scale, they are only entrusted with the simpler tasks which don't need much initiative. Indeed, the pair don't even know why they've been sent to Birmingham, and don't waste time in surmise. The orders will come in good time.

The play is thus the sum total of the desultory conversational ploys and pauses with which the pair while away the intervening hours, until the sudden, unnerving descent of the dumb waiter into their basement. [141] This makes a beautiful moment in the theatre, poised teetering between terror and bathos, disturbing, as it does, their disputes about whether Gus saw Aston Villa beaten in a cup-tie here years ago, [131–3] or whether one should properly say "light the kettle" or "light the gas". [135–6] The orders sent down in the dumb waiter, although they are for meals rather than murders, are treated with great seriousness by Ben and Gus—but with increasing despair as their ad hoc offerings of eccles cakes, potato crisps and bars of chocolate prompt the powers upstairs to make demands for ever more exotic dishes.

At last, the pair having gone over their instructions one last time, the speaking-tube informs Ben that the night's victim is about to enter: he tries to call Gus, who has gone to the lavatory off left—but it is Gus himself who stumbles in from the right-hand entrance "stripped of his jacket, waistcoat, tie, holster and revolver . . . body stooping, his arms at his sides". [159] Ben's revolver is levelled at him, according to his orders: there is a long silence as the two stare at each other, and the curtain falls.

Without a doubt this is Pinter's least complicatedly comic play. Ben's credulous belief in what he reads in his newspaper, his occasional stabs at textbook phraseology, and, most hilarious of all, the pair's frantic theorising about the upstairs cafe, and their attempts to match the variety of its menu—all these ingredients keep the "menace" well below surface for most of the time. The play's opening is more assured, as if Pinter were more certain of his power to compel attention without an immediate plunge into dialogue, than in either of the earlier plays. Gus is simply tying up his shoe-laces, while Ben, lying reading his paper, becomes increasingly engrossed in his colleague's activities as Gus removes one shoe after the other—to extract first a flattened match-box, then a flattened cigarette-packet. He shakes the packet and examines it, Pinter directs, and stamps off to the lavatory. [123]

Considerable attention is paid to the whereabouts of this lavatory, as it is also to the layout of the basement and its decoration—right down to an old cricketing photograph on the wall. Gus "wouldn't like to live in this dump".

> I wouldn't mind if you had a window, you could see what it looked like outside . . . I mean, you come into a place when it's still dark, you come into a room you've never seen before, you sleep all day, you do your job, and then you go away in the night again . . . I like to look at the scenery. You never get the chance in this job. [128]

A place, and the purpose of its mysterious visitors: here is a re-statement of that dominant theme of each of Pinter's first three plays. True, his touch is here of the lightest—and faults of over-explicitness, such as Ben's prolonged repetition of the speaking tube's complaints to the management, [149–50] are few and far between. But behind the chatter about the quality of the china, beyond the search for substitutes for scampi, there is a vein of seriousness that touches and tempers *The Dumb Waiter* at several points.

There are two dumb waiters in the play: the non-speaking service lift, and the bovine Gus, whose business, as Ben has to remind him, is also, unquestioningly, to wait.

GUS: What for?
BEN: For Wilson.
GUS: He might not come. He might just send a message. He doesn't always come. [138]

This verbal echo of *Godot* is no doubt a deliberate parody, and not to be taken too seriously. What becomes much more serious, for Gus, is his insistence on finding such niggling fault with the order of things as he finds them. Somewhere there is a boss, who issues orders, which it is Gus's duty to carry out: that is all he knows in Birmingham, and all he needs to know.

Yet he remains dissatisfied—complaining about the bed and the basement itself, [127] wondering who clears up after the job's been done, [141] and, increasingly, bothered about the job itself. "Don't you ever get a bit fed up?" he asks Ben. [128] Ben doesn't: he even takes the injunctions of the dumb waiter in his stride. Not so his companion:

What's he doing it for? We've been through our tests, haven't we? We got right through our tests, years ago, didn't we? We've proved ourselves before now, haven't we? We've always done our job. What's he doing all this for? What's the idea? What's he playing these games for? [156]

The methodology behind this speech is typical of Pinter. The pervasive mystery becomes more mysterious by being reduced to commonplace terms of tests and qualifications, whilst the particular mystery is also heightened because Gus himself shares the mystification. And it is *because* Gus expresses his doubts so freely that he is being put to the test. He even dares to be inquisitive about who the evening's victim is going to be. [139] The form of the dramatic irony is, as ever, a precise predicate to its content.

Without the hindsight of a first acquaintance with the play, Gus's imminent death at the fall of the curtain is pointless—indeed, it amounts to a vulgarisation of the whole action, a cheap device to twist the tail for the sake of twisting the tail. Once again, it is only when one has got the message in its entirety that one can look at it properly line by line—and realise, for example, *why* Ben and Gus are so very different in character. It is *always* Gus who asks the probing questions, *always* Ben who by-passes them, or tells Gus, more or less vehemently, to shut up. Because of this, one gets the feeling that he "knows something"—that he has been entrusted with more information than Gus, precisely because he accepts it, as he accepts everything he is asked to do, without question. (Such an interpretation illuminates Ben's unnaturally quick reassurance of Gus when the dumb waiter first makes its appearance, [142] as it does his roadside halt for no good reason while Gus was asleep on the way: [129–30] so that whilst Ben doesn't know that Gus is to be his victim until the last moment, he knows that he knows *more* than Gus.)

I wouldn't be so insistent about the difference between the two men, had not most critics talked of Ben and Gus as more or less interchangeable.[22] They are not: if one really looks at what Gus does and says, one could not be at all sure that, if he found himself in Ben's situation as the curtain fell, he would really duly kill his comrade-in-arms. One is in no doubt at all that this is precisely what Ben means to do: and he must do it *because*, in Ben's position, Gus might have disobeyed his orders.[23]

Each of Pinter's earliest plays becomes more terrifying the more one is aware that, if any action is inexorable, this is only because the element of free-will is *there* but is being ignored. Petey *could* have stopped Goldberg and McCann from abducting Stanley. Gus *could* have taken his dissatisfaction one step further, and opted out: or, alternatively, he might have passed his last-chance test and, by accepting the dumb waiter and its orders as readily as Ben, thus have given himself over as completely as his companion to the "organisation".

The racial implications of *The Birthday Party* make it reasonable to think of the "organisation" behind Goldberg and McCann as a quasi-fascist one: and maybe, just as irony is added to such an interpretation by that play's reversal of racial roles, it's also impossible—indeed, paradigmatically, helpful—to think of the crooks of *The Dumb Waiter* as the tools of some civil or religious establishment that demands absolute obedience. Certainly, the oracular nature of the dumb waiter's injunctions makes a religious interpretation tempting. But *The Dumb Waiter* is much less explicit in this respect than *The Birthday Party*—not in its physical and personal details, which are as rich yet down-to-earth as ever, but in the greater opacity of its theme.

It is, curiously, an opposite tendency—a tendency to pin down purposes, instead of teasing them allusively out of the dialogue—to which Pinter seemed to be giving in in his next two plays, as he was also to give in to the temptation to self-parody. *A Slight Ache* and *A Night Out* venture for the first time over the domestic thresholds which at once protect and threaten to stifle the characters of *The Room*, *The Birthday Party* and *The Dumb Waiter*. But these three earliest plays, whilst keeping advisedly within Pinter's artistic limitations, remain remarkably successful explorations of a claustrophobic mood and theme—whether the claustrophobia is that of the clammy refuge from black strangers on the street, of the concentration camp, or of the cell in which the questioning monk agonises over his vow of obedience. None of those images encases its respective play in an adequate nutshell: but the images are *there*, as is much more besides. The beauty of the plays is that their three rooms *are* microcosmic, but that they are also, quite concretely, just three rooms.

2

Explanations and Definitions

A Slight Ache, A Night Out and the Revue Sketches

WHAT DO I MEAN by definitions? In brief, my argument in this chapter is that *A Slight Ache* and *A Night Out* are among Pinter's least interesting plays because, instead of remaining content with *giving definition* to a situation or relationship, this earlier, photographically exact emotional focus is befuzzed by an over-exposure of cause and effect—in short, of explanation. In startling contrast, especially since they are of the same period, the short revue sketches to which Pinter was at this time turning his hand are models of clarity—instant insights into the pokier corners of urban life. Definitions.

Suddenly, in *A Slight Ache*, Pinter moved out of town and, to begin with, out of doors. The action of the play—first broadcast in July 1959, but produced at the Arts Theatre early in 1961 and, in its printed version, scripted as for stage performance—opens as Edward and Flora exchange patio-style breakfast-time pleasantries about gardening, trap a wasp in a jar of marmalade, and prepare to enjoy "the longest day of the year". [14] But the summery mood is suddenly overcast when Edward notices that an ancient and scruffy matchseller has taken up his stand at their back gate, just as he has been doing for weeks past—inexplicably, for the lane running past the gate leads only to a monastery, and Edward has not seen the old man make a single sale.

Flora evidently finds the Matchseller's ubiquitous presence much less objectionable—or at least less threatening—than her husband, who even retreats into the gloom of the scullery to avoid him: but it is at Edward's bidding that he is invited into the house. The old man shuffles indoors, speaking not a word—indeed, he remains absolutely silent throughout the play. In the radio version, of course, this left his very existence in doubt. But since to postulate some shared fantasy or hallucination would be to introduce yet another convention into a play that already employs too many—and since the Matchseller is undeniably, physically *there* in any stage production, for his movements are clearly indicated in the directions—his solidity, if not his reality, must necessarily be accepted.

The rest of the action intersperses one-way interrogations of the Matchseller by Edward with a much more sympathetic attempt by Flora to break down his reserve. She succeeds, as might be expected, only in breaking down her own. Edward, too, gets increasingly, hypnotically unnerved by the insistent silence of the Matchseller, until he himself mumbles into incoherence. "With a great, final effort—a whisper," he asks "Who are you?" [39] And Flora, entering, answers on his behalf: he is called Barnabas, the canopy has been put up for him on the lawn, the house has been polished for him. She hands the tray of matches to her broken husband, and goes out with the Matchseller into the garden.

Edward's one-way interrogations are fine studies in a compulsive resort to triviality which compels revelation, and the "dialogue"—for the old man's responses are interpreted by Edward as his own train of thought suggests—moves through distinct yet inconspicuously jointed phases. From a man-to-man opening, the tones-of-voice Edward adopts are successively cajoling, hectoring, stern, sarcastic, and, finally, confessional. The opening scene on the patio is excellent— the hunting of the wasp at once comic in its overblown intensity, yet vaguely threatening in the minuscule murder, the squashing upon the plate, which is its climax. Quite a heated disagreement about whether wasps "bite" or "sting", [11 and 13] reminiscent of Ben and Gus's semantic squabbles in *The Dumb Waiter*, makes an amusing set-piece. And the passages of dream-like poetic insight in Edward's reminiscing both compel and disturb towards the end of the play:

> I could stand on the hill and look through my telescope at the sea. And follow the path of the three-masted schooner, feeling fit, well aware of my sinews, their suppleness, my arms lifted holding the telescope, steady, easily, no trembling, my aim was perfect, I could pour hot water down the spoon-hole, yes, easily, no difficulty, my grasp firm, my command established, my life was accounted for, I was ready for my excursions to the cliff, down the path to the back gate, through the long grass, no need to watch for the nettles, my progress was fluent, after my long struggling against all kinds of usurpers, disreputables, lists, literally dozens of people anxious to do me down, and my reputation down, my command was established, all summer I would breakfast, survey my landscape, take my telescope, examine the overhanging of my hedges, pursue the narrow lane past the monastery, climb the hill, adjust the lens . . . watch the progress of the three-masted schooner, my progress was as sure, as fluent. . . . [36]

The malleability of the interlocking imagery here, the fusion of person and places, begins to suggest a transcendent image of homes-as-castles that the play might have developed. Instead, the progress of its action is too often that of a symbol-hunt, its clues carefully planted.

Thus, the "slight ache" of the title is an actual ache, in Edward's eyes, [12] but the connection between this nagging irritation and his fear of the Matchseller—the slight ache in his life, of course, for so many weeks past—is at first common-place, [18] and in the end just monstrously inappropriate. For the gothicky horror of the old man—the fungus Edward finds on his tray of matches, [26] the cowl-like business with his balaclava, [37] the vampiric climax as the old man seems to suck vicarious life from a degenerating Edward—is a tangible thing, a matter of the textures of clothes and of flesh. And the whole bias of the play is naturalistic, the ready explanations coming common-sensically:

Edward—listen—he's not here through any . . . design, or anything, I know it. I mean, he might just as well stand outside our back gate as anywhere else. He'll move on. I can . . . make him. I promise you. There's no point in upsetting yourself like this. He's an old man, weak in the head . . . that's all. [28–9]

Is Flora right? If so, how can she make him move on? And why doesn't she keep her promise?

I think the play's crucial weakness may well lie in this under-development of Flora. If her final adoption of the old man, and rejection of her husband, is no more than a figment of Edward's imagination—the slight ache in the eyes deteriorating into total blindness—then Flora's earlier and indisputably "real" behaviour remains unaccounted for: but if the Matchseller has truly cast his spell, or let a spell be cast, over wife as well as husband, then one needs the chance of seeing more of Flora's own developing relationship with the old man than their actual two-or-three page encounter, during which she inches from little politenesses to heavy verbal petting.

Pinter's perfunctory yet, for these reasons, too precise portrayal of Flora is characteristic of his treatment of sexually attractive women. With the Rose Hudds and the Megs, the Mother in *A Night Out*, or the old aunts of *Night School*, he is certain, alike in repulsion or sympathy. With Lulu, with Flora, with the more professional tarts of *A Night Out* and *Night School*, and, most notably, with Ruth in *The Homecoming*, a stereotyped sexual sensibility seems to shimmer over each character's personality. And when, as here, such a woman takes one of the only two speaking parts in the play, the distortion is relatively the more dangerous.

Most of Pinter's plays are full of bits and pieces of fragmented action which have little to do with the plotting of the piece, but a lot to do with the manners and moods of its characters. Here, the action is broken into two segments, cleanly separated by the arrival of the Matchseller. The first part of the play, before the old man's personal appearance, is a good first attempt at exposing an upper middle-class couple in well-off rural surroundings to the kind of surgical probing into language, motives and communication which had tingled lesser-bred nerve-ends in the earlier plays. The nagging arguments over the flower borders are irresistible, and the logic of Edward's

> I don't see why I should be expected to distinguish between these plants. It's not my job. [10]

is as precisely off-the-point in its testiness as anything that Meg says for the sake of saying it. But if the random drinks-list later offered to the Matchseller by Edward [25] is good for an easy laugh, the dwelling upon the exotic brand names in this nervous good-wine guide never becomes part of the man as do-it-yourselfery, for example, becomes so vividly a part of Mick in *The Caretaker*. Neither is Edward's profession —he writes "theological and philosophical essays" [23]— ever inimitably *his*, as, say, looking after deck chairs is part of Petey in *The Birthday Party*.

And by comparison with the down-to-earthness of Goldberg and McCann—or even of the blind Negro—the retributive functioning of the Matchseller seems almost solipsistic. He reminds Flora, predictably, of the poacher who raped her in her girlhood—"long before the flood" [30]—and to Edward he is

My oldest acquaintance. My nearest and dearest. My kith and kin. But surely correspondence would have been as satisfactory . . . more satisfactory? We could have exchanged postcards, couldn't we? What? Views, couldn't we? [36]

How much less poised is the deliberate banality here: and how much sharper is the division between the recognisable, cliché-laden idiom and that vague intimation of embodied mortality to which it is addressed—a gap the phrase "kith and kin" attempts obviously and unsatisfactorily to bridge. Riley in *The Room* may have been Death, but he was also a blind Negro: whether the Matchseller is Something Nasty in the Woodshed, an Anti-Life Force, a Slight Ache, or Death in a more middle-class image, he is never just a Matchseller.[24]

A Slight Ache, then, is at once more explicit and more opaque than any of Pinter's earlier works. In it there is an over-refinement of many techniques he had previously employed, but which here savour of pre-programmed—one might call it compinterised—writing: the familiar manner has been switched on, but the vision, the dramatic energy, is lacking. If *The Caretaker* is, among other things, about two brothers and a tramp, *A Slight Ache* suffers badly from never being about a middle-class couple and a matchseller. It is all symbol and no substance, with quite a few footnotes thrown in to make up the weight.

A Night Out was written for radio, and first broadcast in March 1960, but it has also been televised and staged. Maybe it is to television that it is best suited: one feels the need for some sort of visual embellishment, and yet, during the party scene in particular, a need also for more variation of focus than would be possible in a theatre. However, the first act—there are three altogether, though the play has a total length not much greater than that of *A Slight Ache*—opens familiarly enough, as Albert Stokes, an insignificant, thirtyish clerk, does his best to evade the attentions of his mother, and to overcome her adamant refusal to register that tonight he will be going out to an office party. For Albert to go out at all is evidently unusual, and it becomes apparent during the following scene that he is regarded by his friends, Seeley and Kedge, who have arranged to meet him by a coffee stall, as something of a mother's boy.

In the second act, the party goes disastrously for Albert, who is systematically got at by Gidney, the firm's resident bully, teased by the typists, and eventually accused by one of them of "touching her". [66] The good-natured Seeley defends Albert against Gidney's threatening bluster, but a scuffle ensues, and Albert slams out. Returning home, he is greeted, predictably, by his mother's recriminations—no doubt he's been "mucking about with girls". [71] Albert, got at on all sides, lunges threateningly towards his mother with the kitchen clock, and the second act ends. In *A Slight Ache* the Matchseller's silence had provoked Edward to violence: here it is Albert, silent but simmering, who can no longer endure the flow of maternal monologue.

The play's long penultimate scene takes place later the same night, in the room of a prostitute who has picked up Albert as he gravitates back to the closed coffee-stall. The two swop morale-boosting fantasies until the girl's pernickety concern to keep the cigarette ash off her carpet, too reminiscent of the motherly nagging Albert thought to have escaped, drives him into a second frenzy: he terrorises the girl for a while—indulging in petty bossing-about rather than overtly sexual assertion—then leaves. Returning home, he finds his mother, on whom the impending blow had evidently not fallen after all, waiting up for him—reproachful, forgiving, overwhelming. Like most nights out, this, too, has arrived at its morning after.

A Night Out is at once Pinter's most diffuse and most superficial play. Little bits could sometimes be lopped off and turned into self-sufficient sketches—indeed, the would-be technical discussion between Seeley and Kedge about the previous Saturday's football match actually borrows the coffee-stall setting of *Last to Go*, one of Pinter's sketches for *Pieces of Eight*—and the Old Man who keeps interrupting to pass on a trifling message from Stanley is superfluous except as light relief. Moreover, the profusion of widely-separated settings—kitchen, coffee-stall, the house where the party is being held, and the girl's room—is unique in Pinter's early work. The intention is presumably to show how impossible it is for Albert to escape from his mother's clutches even when he has shaken off her attentions in the flesh. The party confronts him with his own impotence, and the prostitute tries to subject him to the same perfunctory humiliations as his mother.

c

Albert's attempt to assert himself over this apparently more available girl is reminiscent of Stanley's mini-persecution of Meg in *The Birthday Party*: but she proves to be no more within Albert's sexual reach than was Lulu in the earlier play. *A Night Out* has, indeed, far too many muted echoes of its predecessors: and the bossing-about of a sexually feared woman by a man actually lacking in self-assurance was to be a theme varied yet again in Walter's campaign for and against Sally in *Night School*—and in Lenny's opening gambits against Ruth in *The Homecoming*. The psychological truth in such situations decreases as one tends increasingly to react towards them as towards a sort of theatrical tic of their author's. Similarly, the girl herself is typical of Pinter's shabby-genteel prostitutes, and less interesting even than the typists at the office party: her resemblances to Albert's mother are over-stressed, too, making his failure and fury with her a special case, instead of the indelible character-trait they would have seemed had (say) one of Gidney's girls taken him home instead.

A Night Out can come dangerously near to dependence upon a particularly unsubtle form of tension in its penultimate scene. But different directors for different media have been less concerned than Pinter with suggesting that Albert is indeed about to stun his mother, or worse, at the close of the second act. On the handling of that earlier moment will depend an unfamiliar audience's feelings as Albert makes veiled hints to the prostitute about what he has done, and as he slouches luxuriously home, only to freeze back into apathy at the sound of his mother's voice. Whether he has been fantasising all along is irrelevant, as indeed is any particular interpretation put upon the business with the clock once one *knows*, having seen or read the play for a first time, that his gesture has been either thwarted or ineffectual. So that whereas one returns to most of Pinter's work ready to add to what one knows already, here the apparent intention to deceive irritates at second sight if it fooled at first—and even if it doesn't, it becomes merely a matter for the observance of a particular director's technique, not a turning point of the play.

Albert's failure to kill his mother—just as Stanley had failed to strangle Meg in *The Birthday Party*—nevertheless encourages him to exercise a little brief authority. From this, however, he learns nothing. Christy Mahon, hero of Synge's *Playboy of the Western World*, came from another convention of comedy altogether. His character was shaped by experience, and his intention of patricide at least loosened the tie of the overall-strings. Back among the lower-to-lower-middle classes Pinter is certainly a lot happier showing characters leaving events unscathed than he was in the stockbroker-belted *Slight Ache*: but the formula is the same, and although its components are turned with professional assurance, the end product no longer carries the same conviction or, frankly, the same interest.

The best things in *A Night Out* are those that promise well for the future—the sharpening of the blunter-edged minor characters, for example. The compinterised call-girl apart, these are as surprisingly successful as they are numerous, from the pettily ceremonious Mr King, senior-partnering it at the party, to Albert's best and apparently only friend, Seeley—whose defence of his persecuted pal against the unspeakable but (in a lounge-bar lingeringly sort of way) recognisable Gidney [68–9] adds a note of hesitancy to the action just where it is needed, as did Petey's intervention in *The Birthday Party*. Indeed, the play would have been better for a more liberal dose of Seeley or Petey's sense of free-will, such as to make Albert's loss or rejection of it all the more dispiriting.

The Mother is much better drawn than Albert himself. Her cloying possessiveness is more cunning than Meg's: its armpitty odour is one of carbolic soap rather than stewed tea-leaves, and her home is not sluttish like Meg's—yet the more suffocating in that it is "clean and tidy", its meals regular, its chairs comfortable. [43] But the oedipal-cum-proprietary interest is the same, the instincts of love and of domination similarly confused. At first wilfully refusing to pay any attention to Albert's repeated statements that he is going out, his mother gets at him with all her armoury of domestic small shot—dinners that will be spoiled, ties that ought to be pressed, light bulbs that need fixing. These verbal motifs recur throughout the play, burned into Albert's consciousness like brands signifying a guilt he knows he need not feel, yet which he can't eradicate.

The speeches in the play which linger in the memory are those in which such damaged household goods are reshuffled yet again into the dialogue of mother or son—as here, in the former's parting reproaches to the partygoing Albert.

Well, what am I going to do while you're out? I can't go into Grandma's room because there's no light. I can't go down to the cellar in the dark, we were going to have a game of cards, it's Friday night, what about our game of rummy? [48]

And Albert, at the height of his fury with the prostitute, reaches back to just such minor irritants:

You're all the same, you see, you're all the same, you're just a dead weight round my neck. What makes you think . . . What makes you think you can . . . tell me . . . yes . . . It's the same as this business about the light in Grandma's

room. Always something. Always something . . . My ash?
I'll put it where I like! You see this clock? Watch your
step. Just watch your step. [83]

And he threatens her, too, with the clock, his mind picking
over all the other pinpricked sores of the evening—Gidney's
taunts about his lack of qualifications, for example:

I've got as many qualifications as the next man. Let's get
that quite . . . straight. And I got the answer to her, you
see, tonight . . . I finished the conversation . . . I finished
it . . . I finished her. [83]

But both speeches become flawed as they stumble into one's
doubts about what *did* happen just after the second-act
curtain.

I don't think one's wish for certainty on this point is a
symptom of that "desire for verification" which, in Pinter's
words, "cannot always be satisfied".[25] For here Pinter has
set up his own situation and established his own premises—
and in this play, as in *A Slight Ache*, the ostensible naturalism
is exploited too hard to be thus wilfully abnegated. Gidney's
motives for getting at Albert, and his methods of so doing, are
slender indeed, yet both are elaborately "verified". And the
mechanics of the trick itself are carefully worked out, right
down to the stage direction that it "must be quite clear from
the expression" of Mr Ryan—the bland, speechless old man
whose retirement the party is supposed to be honouring—
that he is really the one who has "interfered" with Eileen.
[67]

The explicitness here is in sharp contrast with the
unfocused menace of Goldberg and McCann, and although
something of a more specific kind is demanded by the whole

ambience of the play—which is more objectified and every-day in its assumptions than *The Birthday Party*—Pinter isn't any too happy in getting it across. Thus, Mr Ryan's total silence throughout the party is a slight ache to enact on stage, though it stylises well enough on television. But *why* is he silent? And *why* is it so necessary to pin the blame on him? What difference would it have made if we'd been left wondering whether or not Albert was any better at touching up a typist than at knocking down his mother?

Albert's sensitivity to any mention of his mother's name, let alone to any hint of his dependence upon her, is over-emphatic too: in particular, the attempt to externalise the mother-son relationship by having Seeley and Kedge dredge it up over their coffee strikes one as apologetic. And when even the girl tells Albert that there's "something childish in your face, almost retarded", [81] the inadequate dramatising of the relationship as it is manifested to such outsiders strikes one more forcefully: though at the same time it occurs to one that this is Pinter's first attempt to set his own living-womb world within a relatively "normal" outside context.

A Night Out is thus a more ambitious play than *A Slight Ache* because for the first time Pinter is attempting to inter-pose his own set of strangers between an eccentric situation and its audience in a theatre. Instead of being able to enter the world of the main characters—in this case, of Albert, his mother, and the girl—at one step, one has therefore to tread an intermediate path through the slightly more familiar world in which Seeley, Kedge and Gidney measure out their own and Albert's working lives at Messrs Hislop, King and Martindale. But the more these intermediary characters amuse themselves by psychologising Albert, the more an audience seems invited to do so—and the clearer the impossibility of conceiving him in quasi-naturalistic terms becomes.

Similarly, in forcing his parallel between the Mother and the prostitute, Pinter slips an unnecessary piece of symbolism into the action: the photograph of the "daughter"—which turns out to be one of the girl herself, and thus to represent the Mother's wish for identification with the child, and her denial of an independent existence to Albert. But instead of clarifying the issue, this generalising process again confuses it. It may be significant that after *A Night Out* Pinter was not to cast his socialising net so wide again until, in *Landscape*, he had evolved a subtler means of giving his characters a specific and identifiable worldly context.

But although his longer plays were to retreat back within four walls, Pinter did continue, more happily, to develop the knack of capturing random rather than eccentric samples of society in a few careful strokes. The result was that series of delicate miniatures which, for want of a better term, must be dubbed the revue-sketches they became during 1959, in *One to Another* and in *Pieces of Eight*. Yet the carefully structured three acts of *A Night Out* seem anecdotal and superficial by comparison with these—and the psychology of several of the sketches precise and, in depth of human insight, even profound.

The most orthodoxly sketch-like sketches are the least happy. *Trouble in the Works* takes the form of an interview between Wills, a shop steward, and his boss, Fibbs. There's "been a little trouble in the factory", because, as Wills is coaxed into revealing, the men "seem to have taken a turn against some of the products". [119] What follows is little more than a catalogue of complicated sounding spare parts—hemi unibal spherical rod ends, and suchlike—elaborated into a deeply-felt conversation between the two men. The style is more reminiscent of N. F. Simpson than of Pinter himself, and the humour derives in part from the quick-fire interchange of mechanical jargon as such, and in part from the disproportionate awe and distaste with which boss and workers respectively regard their products. When a blackout line is needed, Wills tells a broken Fibbs that what the men really want is to make brandy balls. [121] Paul Jennings is much better at playing off spherical rod ends against parallel male stud couplings, and, although the sketch is good for a few non-recognition laughs, it strikes one as a hasty, pot-boiling effort.

Applicant, also a two-hander in the interview format, is evidently more ambitious. A young physicist applying for a job is put through "a little test to determine his psychological suitability" by a languid young female executive. [131] Bedecked with electrodes and earphones, the applicant is reduced to a state of collapse by a sequence of non-sequential questions very similar to the sort which Goldberg and McCann fired at Stanley Webber. Here, the victim gives a rather better account of himself, but, as in *Trouble in the Works*, the absence of context or of any conceivable purpose prevents the sketch from working once its instantaneous impact has been made: and in re-reading it quickly palls.[26]

Of course, for any revue sketch to outlive its after-dinner purpose, let alone by more than the few months before its manner or its matter become dated, is rare indeed: and this makes the enduring quality of the remaining three readily available sketches[27] all the more remarkable—although some did originate as the plays-in-miniature they now seem, for which no vehicle other than that of intimate revue happened to be theatrically appropriate.[28] In these, Pinter abandons the lazy-zany humour of *Trouble in the Works* and *Applicant*, and explores three of the more strangely-familiar corners of London life.

Request Stop, the shortest of the three, is virtually a monologue, in which a woman waiting for a bus harangues an inoffensive neighbour in the queue who may or may not have been "making insinuations" in response to her enquiry about getting a bus to Shepherds Bush. The piquancy of the situation lies, of course, as much in the uncomfortable non-reactions of the rest of the queue as in the woman's stream of accusations—which become inextricably mixed up with all her prejudices against "foreigners", among whom the little man is sure to be numbered. The sketch is flawed by straining too hard for its punch-line, but its fuzzy illogic finely counterpoints the woman's total self-assurance, and the embarrassed shiver of recognition is genuine.

The Black and White and *Last to Go* both drag their short lengths along at night, the first in a cheap milk bar near Fleet Street, the second at a coffee stall. Superficially, both are exercises in non-communication, their comedy dependent upon the non-sequiturs, back-tracking, and sheer inconsequence of the conversations—between two old women in the first sketch, and the barman and a newspaper seller just finished for the night in the second. Yet even non-communication has its finer shades. The meeting in *The Black and White* is a kind of regular, relished ritual for its dowdy old night birds, who seem to be forever drifting off along all-night bus routes to other havens of tea and temporary warmth:

SECOND: I'm going. I'm going up to the Garden.
FIRST: I'm not going down there. *Pause.* I'm going up to Waterloo Bridge.
SECOND: You'll just about see the last two-nine-six come up over the river.
FIRST: I'll just catch a look of it. Time I get up there.
Pause.

It don't look like an all-night bus in daylight, do it? [125]

Night haunts and the times of the buses *matter* to these old girls: and if they repeat themselves, it is because they want to be sure their points have been appreciated. One can foresee that the sight of that last two-nine-six passing along the Embankment in broad daylight is going to be avidly recounted in the early-hours meeting on the following morning.

Neither the barman nor his customer in *Last to Go*, on the other hand, is in the least interested in what the other is saying. The main subject of their "conversation" is the impossibility of predicting whether the *Star*, *News* or *Standard* will be the last of the evening's papers to be sold:

No way of telling beforehand. Until you've got your last one left, of course. Then you can tell which one it's going to be. [130]

Comment would be superfluous: but then practically every comment in the sketch is superfluous. Within four pages of script one knows these people as one never knew the outsiders in *A Night Out* in forty.

The Black and White and *Last to Go* are particularly important to Pinter's development in that—although they represent that close observation of the inconsequential which is most frequently thought of as the essence of the "pinteresque"—they are in fact his only excursions into unqualified realism: for even *The Caretaker* is *shaped*, albeit naturalistically, by its beginning, middle and end. The definition these sketches give to their characters and situations is total: and yet, in contrast to the heavily-glossed *Slight Ache* and *Night Out*, they *explain* nothing. After the housebound allegories of his first three plays, Pinter's ventures outdoors thus proved successful only when, in these two revue sketches in particular, every hint of a symbol had been stripped away. Perhaps in consequence, he was able, in the plays which followed, to infuse into three more domestic interiors a much richer sense of the outside world—not merely as a vague, womb-invading threat, but as an actual modifying influence upon the indoors-action, And, after the total inability of Edward in *A Slight Ache* or of Albert in *A Night Out* to alter their fates by a single spiritual inch, it is refreshing to find the element of free-will in *The Caretaker*, *Night School* and *The Dwarfs* not only a possibility hovering in the background, but an active ingredient of the plays. In each of them, choices are confronted, and decisions, for better or worse, are made.

3

Acceptances and Rejections

The Caretaker, Night School and The Dwarfs

PINTER'S WORK has felt its way towards and beyond realism. *The Room* and *The Birthday Party* were allusive and allegorical. *The Dumb Waiter* was slightly more precise both in its symbolism and its substance: then, the "need for verification" evidently proving irresistible, *A Slight Ache* over-explained itself in metaphysical terms, as did *A Night Out* in physical. But, before he wrote *The Caretaker*, only in the revue sketches had Pinter attempted and achieved the realism in which action is shaped by past or present experience, and to which any objectified significance or internal coherence is occasional and accidental. After the lessons of *The Caretaker* had been assimilated, the dramatic process became increasingly for Pinter one of fining down reality, instead, as previously, of embellishing it. This makes *The Caretaker* in many ways the easiest of his plays to understand, though not necessarily either better or worse for this ready accessibility. As it happened, however, the play was long to remain a peak as well as a turning-point in Pinter's creative career.

First produced at the Arts Theatre Club in April 1960, and quickly moved into the Duchess for a long and successful run, *The Caretaker* exploits a basically simple situation—just as it was sparked-off in Pinter's mind by his casual

conversations ("he did most of the talking") with one particular tramp.[29] Aston, a man in his early thirties living in a
single, compulsively cluttered room in an otherwise derelict
house, comes to the rescue of an old tramp who's got himself
involved in a brawl, and good-naturedly offers him a bed
while he's getting himself "sorted out". [16] The tramp's
real name is Davies—though for no apparent reason he has
been going around under the assumed name of Bernard
Jenkins. The habitual, instinctive evasiveness this typifies is
ingrained deep in the old man's character—and his ready
suspicions quicken when he finds out that the house really
belongs to Aston's younger brother, Mick, on whose charity
Davies at first finds it less easy to batten.

Encouraged by Mick's offer of a caretaking job, however
—and disconcerted by Aston's revelation that he has undergone electric shock treatment in a mental hospital—the
tramp shifts his allegiance, doing all he can to confirm Mick's
apparent misgivings about his brother. But this proves to be
playing into Mick's hands. Davies tries to assert his supposed
superiority to Aston, who calmly but insistently shows him
the door. As Mick had evidently intended, the eviction,
though of his own engineering, is by his brother's choice.
As the curtain falls, Davies is pleading with an impassive
Aston to let him stay.

Most critics seem to have taken it for granted that Aston's
mind is made up, and the weight of evidence certainly points
that way. But as it stands the play nevertheless ends incon-
clusively: and it is important that it should do so.[30] All the
decisions have yet to be taken. Will Davies ever make his
much-discussed, always avoided trip down to Sidcup, to
collect the "papers" that prove his identity? Will Aston
get started on that shed in the garden he has been meaning
to build? I think it's too easy to overlay either or both of these

unfulfilled aims with a fatalistic symbolism: after all, the building of the shed *would* be a tangible and effective expression of Aston's ability to get to grips with things again— and the tramp's trip to Sidcup has its measurable mileage from Shepherds Bush, where the action seems to be set. Thus, the unlikelihood of Davies's ever setting off there is due not to any godotesque elusiveness about the southern suburbs of London, but to the tramp's own preference for procrastination.

Unlike, say, Edward in *A Slight Ache*, neither Davies nor Aston has been denied free-will: and that the action ends with all the options open is significant. It connects with the play's episodic quality—for its three acts are unusually (and some have thought disruptively) fragmented into short scenes —and with the related sense of *drifting*, whether in the actual movements of the characters on and off stage or in their gradually realigning relationships. *The Caretaker* simply deals, as Pinter has said, with "a particular human situation, concerning three particular people, and not, incidentally, . . . symbols".[31]

This was to be the first play in a distinct "period" of Pinter's writing in which shifting power-relationships in a struggle for dominance were to give shape to the action. But it is a mistake to confuse the shape of *The Caretaker* with its substance. True, Pinter had asserted an absolute identification of the two in his short story *The Examination*, which dealt, in his own words,

> with two people in one room having a battle of an unspecified nature, in which the question was one of who was dominant at what point and how they were going to be dominant and what tools they would use to achieve dominance. . . .[32]

But in *The Caretaker* the nature of the battle *is* specified, and the relative strengths of the antagonists are never really in doubt. Mick can play Davies like a fish, and if he wanted to land him could do so at any moment. Indeed, as soon as Davies agrees to become Mick's caretaker instead of Aston's the issue is as good as settled. Caretaking, keeping things ticking over—as in the title of *The Dumb Waiter*, a pun, intentional or not, is present and suggestive—is not much in Mick's line. It is very much in Aston's.

The entire action takes place in Aston's junk shop of a room, and all his useless bits and pieces, which may or may not come in handy, give some solidity to the state of transition—a sort of spiritual camping-out—in which he finds himself. "The other rooms would . . . would be no good to you," he tells Davies: [16] similarly, other people's minds are, for the moment, inaccessible to him. But although Aston is estranged from society, he is not the only outsider in the play. Davies has tried to intrude upon a fraternal relationship—whilst Mick, who lives elsewhere, is a visitor from the world beyond these four walls, a world where a living has to be earned and a business, evidently in the building trade, to be built up.

Naturalistically, Mick's style of verbal bullying—reminiscent of Goldberg's in *The Birthday Party*—is the play's weakest link, and although the *effects* of his wordstorms on Davies are psychologically well-charted, the nerve-nagging device has since become so familiar in contemporary drama that one tends to forget how excessive a stylisation of normal speech behaviour it really is. Mick is thus the most conventionalised character in the play: the racy go-getter, sure of himself and of how to manipulate others, but with that humane—or it might be sentimental—streak that has made him truly his brother's keeper. He is, as Davies tentatively puts it, "a bit of a joker", [39] but his jokes have purpose, and their language has a certain, do-it-yourself poetry:

> You could have an off-white pile linen rug, a table in . . . in afromosia teak veneer, sideboard with matt black drawers, curved chairs with cushioned seats, armchairs in oatmeal tweed, beech frame settee with woven sea-grass seat, white-topped heat resistant coffee table, white tile surround. Yes. [60]

But Mick's eulogies of interior decoration and odes to the bus routes serving Islington [32] are lyrical interludes in what is otherwise Pinter's most successful *narrative* work. And even Mick comes most fully alive when he suddenly shrugs off his pose, and—no doubt only momentarily—combines exasperation and apathy in his closing speech:

> Anyone would think this house was all I got to worry about. I got plenty of other things I can worry about. I've got other things. I've got plenty of other interests. I've got my own business to build up, haven't I? I got to think about expanding . . . in all directions. I don't stand still. I'm moving about, all the time. . . . I've got to think about the future. I'm not worried about this house. I'm not interested. My brother can worry about it. He can do it up, he can decorate it, he can do what he likes with it. I'm not bothered. I thought I was doing him a favour, letting him live here. He's got his own ideas. Let him have them. I'm going to chuck it in. [74]

Mick's language here is strikingly different from those crisp, well-planned strings of sentences he employs elsewhere, full of ready-made, easily connected phrases—not only in his do-it-yourself day-dreaming, but in his careful though seemingly casual swopping of polite commonplaces with Davies.

The tramp's own idiom has more in common with Aston's, just as the characters themselves have more in common, but is nevertheless carefully differentiated from the elder brother's. Davies's evasive instincts urge him into utterly directionless sentences, endless ellipses, meandering that is only meaningful in that it is never intended to get to the point:

> Don't know as these shoes'll be much good. It's a hard road, I been down there before. Coming the other way, like. Last time I left here, it was . . . last time . . . getting on a while back . . . the road was bad, the rain was coming down, lucky I didn't die there on the road, but I got here, I kept going, all along . . . yes . . . I kept going all along. But all the same, I can't go on like this, what I got to do, I got to get back there, find this man— [66]

Aston's short, very simple sentences are also punctuated with many pauses: but these are genuine, often heartfelt searchings for the right way of putting something, or for the logical connection that evades him. There are the gropings for a difficult word, the small shames of substituting a simpler or less precise one, and the triumphs of the remembered, appropriate phrase:

> Then one day they took me to a hospital, right outside London. They . . . got me there. I didn't want to go. Anyway . . . I tried to get out, quite a few times. But . . . it wasn't very easy. They asked me questions, in there. Got me in and asked me all sorts of questions. Well, I told them

... when they wanted to know . . . what my thoughts were. Hmmnn. Then one day . . . this man . . . doctor, I suppose . . . the head one . . . he was quite a man of . . . distinction . . . although I wasn't so sure about that. He called me in. He said . . . he told me I had something. He said they'd concluded their examination. That's what he said. And he showed me a pile of papers and he said that I'd got something, some complaint. He said . . . he just said that, you see. You've got . . . this thing. [55]

This, of course, is from Aston's set speech about his experiences in hospital, at the end of the second act. And, as Pinter himself has emphasised, "it isn't necessary to conclude that everything Aston says about his experiences in the mental hospital is true".[33] But the speech *is* integral to his character, and thus to the play, just as Mick is reliable even in his unreliability, and Davies consistent in his inconsistency. "I can take nothing you say at face value," says Mick. "Every word you speak is open to any number of different interpretations. Most of what you say is lies. You're violent, you're erratic, you're just completely unpredictable." [73] But even this charge needn't be taken at its face value: for Davies is in fact almost pathetically predictable, and Mick is well able to play on this predictability. He is, in fact, probably the character one feels one knows most fully in all of Pinter's plays.

Davies is procrastination personified. But his procrastination really stems from an acute distrust of everybody and everything. He has changed his name for no apparent reason—confiding his real identity to Aston, in the brief burst of grateful confidence that follows his rescue from the fight, but maintaining that he is Bernard Jenkins to the intruding Mick [30–1]—and he is now terrified of being put in prison for having an assumed name on his insurance card. He is, in truth, scared out of his wits by the world around him. Thus, his only fully articulated objection to the caretaking job is that it will expose him to opening the door to strangers:

> They might be there after my card, I mean look at it, here I am, I only got four stamps on this card, that's all I got, I ain't got any more, that's all I got, they ring the bell called Caretaker, they'd have me in, that's what they'd do, I wouldn't stand a chance. Of course I got plenty of other cards lying about, but they don't that, and I can't tell them, can I, because then they'd find out I was going about under an assumed name. [44]

Those papers down in Sidcup, where they were taken for safe keeping "about near on fifteen year ago", [21] are the real, tangible evidences of identity behind which Davies hopes to shield himself from the bureaucrats. But, armed with these, he might very well find himself as defenceless as before: no wonder he prefers to put off the discovery. Sidcup is a last hope only so long as it remains no more than a hope.

Davies has been unable to get to grips with even the commonest conveniences of modern life, preferring not to tamper with Aston's electric fire even though it offers him free warmth, and deeply suspicious of emanations from the disconnected gas cooker which is too close to his bed. [26] Like most such dropouts, he just can't cope with the complicated demands society makes upon him, and so he retreats into his world of evasion—evasion of authority, evasion even of the friendship Aston offers, and of the immaterial confidences it demands:

ASTON: Welsh, are you?

DAVIES: Eh?

ASTON: You Welsh?

Pause.

DAVIES: Well, I been around, you know . . . what I mean
. . . I been about . . . [25]

Note how the avoidance of the direct answer—which in
Stanley's questioning of Lulu about Meg's earlier lodgers
was not only out of character but outside the play's terms of
formal reference—here derives from a recognisable and rigid
habit. The evasion matters not because it mystifies us, but
because it characterises Davies. Thus, habitually suspicious,
he succeeds only in arousing suspicions—asking Aston once
too often for a couple of bob, [26] or, prying around in his
absence, awakening the readier distrust of Mick. [28–9]

Pinter rounds him out with deft little touches of idio-
syncrasy: his dislike of drinking his Guinness from a mug, [19]
his professional preoccupation with shoes, and an unexpected
insistence on his own cleanliness—manifested in his fond
remembrance of the lavatory attendant who "always slipped
me a bit of soap every time I went in there", [13] and his
distaste for his one-time wife's dirty underwear in the vege-
table pan. [9]

Most of the time he succeeds in deceiving himself rather
than others: but just occasionally, when he imagines that he
is in the ascendant, he betrays an unexpected self-knowledge
in offering a home truth to somebody else:

ASTON: Look. If I give you . . . a few bob you can get down
to Sidcup.

DAVIES: You build your shed first! A few bob! When I can
earn a steady wage here! You build your stinking shed
first! That's what! [69]

This is a fatal error, which touches Aston on a sensitive spot. Retaliating, he strikes at Davies's pathetic pride in his cleanliness, telling him he stinks: and the tramp, for the second time in the play, is provoked into a threat of violence, revealing the viciousness that underlies the fear, the prejudice that spawns beneath the feeble keeping-up of appearances.[34]

Davies is violently antipathetic towards "the Blacks", and, for that matter, towards "them aliens" in general—"Poles, Greeks, Blacks, the lot of them". [8] He blames Aston's Indian neighbours for the noises he himself makes in the night, [23] and even convinces himself "about them Blacks coming up from next door, and using the lavatory". [59] It is, moreover, only after Aston reveals that he, too, is "different" that Davies really turns against him. Aston's long confessional at the end of the second act has been much objected to—either because it seems out of tone with the rest of the play, or because it seems unnecessarily definitive in its explanations.[35] As my own criticisms of *A Slight Ache* and *A Night Out* suggest, I'd agree that Pinter has sometimes been guilty of over-explicitness: but not here. Aston's set speech gives centrality and focus to the whole play. It gives an unexpectedly delicate definition to the relationship between the two brothers—explaining the *dramatic* necessity for Mick's intermittent appearances, *taking care* of Aston, which would otherwise be merely functional—and it motivates Davies's intended shift in allegiance. Far from not having listened to Aston's story, as he tells Mick, [59] Davies was, in fact, taking in every word.

Thus, in a sort of antiphony to Aston's confidences, he flings them back into his face in probably the most articulate —certainly the longest—speech he makes in the play. [66–7] And he tells Mick that his brother should "go back where he come from".

MICK: Where did he come from?
DAVIES: Well . . . he . . . he . . .
MICK: You get a bit out of your depth sometimes, don't you? [71]

It's worth noticing that Davies's choice of phrase resonates with racialist echoes: and the tramp, unquestioningly accepted at first by the tolerant Aston, is ultimately rejected because *he* rejects. He is a poor, broken-down old man, an outcast from a society which scares him rigid: and yet, because he is scared, he is also vindictive and, in his spitefulness, hard to forgive. The final act of forgiveness or of condemnation is the audience's, however, for Davies's last appeal has gone unanswered as the curtain falls.

The presence of the tramp, then, refines and clarifies the relationship between the two brothers. It's easy to forget in reading the play one of the theatrical images that comes across with most force—the opening minute, during which Mick "is alone in the room, sitting on the bed, watching". He departs silently as soon as he hears Aston return—as it turns out, with Davies in tow. [7] The residual image serves an important structural purpose as the play progresses. It focuses our attention upon Davies's *reaction* to Mick's return, whereas an intruder previously unseen by the audience would have been a rival centre of dramatic interest. It quietly underscores Mick's claim to ownership of the room —indeed, of the house. And it hints, too, at something conspiratorial between the two brothers. Are their successive offers of a caretaking job to Davies merely coincidental, for example, or part of a pre-arranged plot? And one's sense of a perhaps unspoken conspiracy is heightened again at those moments when it is Davies who becomes most recognisably the outsider—during his interruption of their mutually immersed conversation about tarring over the leak from the roof, [37] and during the final confrontation between Mick and Aston when "they look at each other", and "both are smiling, faintly". [75] The faint smile, the ease with which they can slip into each other's mode of being, suggests the kind of tentative touching which marks their relationship, and which Davies comes between at his peril.

Yet Aston, too, is outsider in his turn, a man who has been rejected as abnormal by society, and who is now struggling painfully back towards contact with it. Does his friendship with Davies represent a step in the right direction, or a regression—a recognition of like by like? Is Mick's concern to engineer the expulsion of Davies therefore a symptom of jealousy, or of genuine concern? Aston himself is enigmatic in his estrangement, yet also more capable of openness than any other character in *The Caretaker*, and transparent even in his conflicts of loyalty. Thus, he's the only participant in the game played by Mick with Davies's bag who's uncertain which side he's on—sorry for the tramp who's being taunted, he is also instinctively loyal to his brother, just as Mick, preserving the probable fiction that Aston is "just about to start" on his redecorating, [36] is instinctively loyal to *him*.

Yet even if Aston is going to need a lot more loyalty, a lot more patience, before he *does* get started, there's no reason whatsoever why he shouldn't. "I like . . . working with my hands," he says, [17] and there is something immensely moving about his vision of the shed that is going to be his workshop:

> Once I get that shed up outside . . . I'll be able to give a bit more thought to the flat, you see. Perhaps I can knock up one or two things for it . . . I can work with my hands, you see. That's one thing I can do. I never knew I could.

But I can do all sorts of things now, with my hands. You know, manual things. When I get the shed up out there ... I'll have a workshop, you see. I ... could do a bit of woodwork. Simple woodwork, to start. Working with ... good wood. [40]

This element of thwarted creativity in *The Caretaker* is the closest Pinter has ever come to talking about Jerusalem. Aston has caught a glimpse of that city in the far distance, and to reach it he has already passed through the valley of the shadow of death:

I couldn't keep ... upright. And I had these headaches. I used to sit in my room. That was when I lived with my mother. And my brother. He was younger than me. And I laid everything out, in order, in my room, all the things I knew were mine, but I didn't die. The thing is, I should have been dead. I should have died. Anyway, I feel much better now. I steer clear of places like that cafe. I never go into them now. I don't talk to anyone ... like that. I've often thought of going back and trying to find the man who did that to me. But I want to do something first. I want to build that shed out in the garden. [57]

When I first saw *The Caretaker* I was convinced that Aston's shed would never be built. Now I am certain that it could be.

The greatness of *The Caretaker* is that it works upon the mind, and goes on working, as, say, the simplistic agonisings of *The Homecoming* never can. Pinter has created three highly idiosyncratic characters who yet aspire to a mythic, universalised status. Hamlet was, after all, the procrastinator *par excellence*: and he, like Aston, had also suffered or feigned madness. If one can push that analogy no further, it is because building a shed is no such great matter as murdering a stepfather—although Aston's mother, like Hamlet's, has betrayed him, and eventually he wants to "find the man who did that to me" with her permission. And Aston gets only a single soliloquy: but that is as integral to the action of *The Caretaker* as are any of Hamlet's to his own tragedy.

Here, there *need* be no tragedy. But there has been suffering, though its pathos has never for one moment been tinged with sentimentality.

And I laid everything out, in order, in my room, all the things I knew were mine, but I didn't die.

One shares Aston's own distance from his behaviour: but it is none the less overwhelming in its pitiful simplicity. One could elaborate Davies into the subtle tempter of a modern morality play, Aston into Everyman, and Mick, presumably, into Mercy—indeed, the thought isn't as fanciful as it sounds, if one recalls the blending of coarse humour with life-or-death struggle in *Mankynd*. But the play is, as Pinter points out, really *about* two brothers and a tramp, just as Hamlet is about a prevaricating prince, his mother and his stepfather. Those are the plays the dramatists wrote: where they left off, the mythmaking begins. And it is precisely because Pinter made the situation of *The Caretaker* so particular, so personalised, that its potential as a myth, capable of entering into the very fabric of the lives of those who have experienced it, is so great.

If *The Caretaker* is a universal play, *Night School* is very much an occasional one. Televised in July 1960, but printed in the version later broadcast on the Third Programme, it is an hour-long anecdote, a comic variation on the acceptances-and-rejections theme as *The Dwarfs* was to be a philosophical one. Walter, by trade a not-very-good petty forger, returns to the home of his Aunts Annie and Milly after a spell in jail. To his dismay, he learns that the old ladies have been letting his room to a young schoolteacher called Sally, whom they have no intention of turning out. "We only got the pension," they explain: [85] besides, Sally is a model tenant, clean and tidy, and out several evenings a week at night school.

Condemned to the "put-u-up" in the dining room, Walter plots to get the girl out as ineptly as he attempts to defraud the post office. He steals a photograph of Sally from among her belongings, which shows that in reality she is a night-club hostess; but instead of taxing her with the discovery, he asks his aunts' man-of-the-world landlord Solto to see if he can find out the name of the club where the girl is currently employed. Sally meanwhile makes overtures of a kind to Walter. Probably he could get both the room and the girl if he tried: but when Solto does run Sally to earth, he's more interested in securing her sexual favours than in solving Walter's mystery. Not having been told that the girl in the photo and the aunts' lodger are one and the same, he even reveals to Sally that it is Walter who has asked him to ferret her out: but he promises not to give away her secret. And so, to the amazement of the aunts and the frustration of Walter, Sally leaves, silently, in the night. Walter will, presumably, get his room back: but, for the first time in one of Pinter's plays this doesn't seem to matter as much as the wilful departure of the outsider.

One critic has complained of *Night School* that "all the ambiguities are resolved completely in a way that offers no surprises".[36] But to demand surprises from Pinter's plays seems to me no less limiting than demanding "verification" when the dramatist chooses not to offer it. It so happens that here the loose-ends are all tied up—but if there is something disquietingly scribean about the pivotal function of the photograph in the plot, the fact that it offers no such twists or teasers as *The Dumb Waiter* or *The Birthday Party* tells us more about Pinter's attitude to playwriting at this stage of his career than it does about the intrinsic merits or demerits of the play.

Arguably, *Night School* is too dense. For example, its glimpses of the shady landlord, Solto, scouring the night clubs and eventually chatting up Sally, are tantalising, for Solto has become fully alive in his self-made seedy way: but they open out the action of the play at rather too late a stage, leaving Walter and his aunts little time to react revealingly to the girl's departure. To see the play mainly in terms of its plot is, however, misleading: if one thinks of it rather as a reshuffling of character relationships, for which the plot provides a deliberately formalised framework, it becomes a much more deftly patterned work. The patterns are, as in *The Caretaker*, of acceptance and rejection: and the play, like so many of Pinter's, is infinitely more rewarding on a second acquaintance precisely because its "surprises" have already been built into our expectations and response.

Intended for television and rewritten for radio though it was, *Night School* would adapt much more readily to stage performance than *A Night Out*. Scenically it could be fitted into a single setting—assuming that the night club scenes were disposed of downstage, with a few suitably suggestive furnishings. A simple domestic interior would then suffice, incorporating the living room, hallway, and disputed bedroom of the aunts' house, for the brief scenes in the old ladies' bedroom could be adapted downstairs with a minimum of textual tampering. More to the point, though, the action is "legitimately" rather than televisually dramatic because it creates its own emphases, whereas those of *A Night Out* often cry out to be decided by the cameras.

With the exception of the scene in the night-club dressing-room, each episode is essentially a cameo in which two or more characters brush fleetingly against one another, in an attempt at confrontation or evasion. The play works by counterpointing the "settled" relationships—between Walter and his aunts, between the aunts and one another, between the aunts and Solto—with those that are unformed, or transformed by circumstances. Walter and Solto, Walter and Sally, Sally and Solto: the three pair up in all these permutations, but never coincide—not because it would upset the plot for them to do so, but because the interest of the separate two-way meetings lies in the shuffling and re-shuffling of identities and attitudes which all three employ to give a particular acquaintance its desired appearance.

By contrast, the aunts know instinctively where they stand. Milly is the dominant one, Annie the one who is dominated but does all the work, and derives some satisfaction from ritual protests against her subordination. They object to Walter's criminality only because it is unremunerative, otherwise treating his absences in prison as an occupational hazard. Here is an early snatch of dialogue:

> WALTER: Well, I'm back now, eh?
> MILLY: How did they treat you this time?
> WALTER: Very well. Very well.
> MILLY: When you going back? [83]

But one has to know the play previously before one can relish the humour of Milly's view of prison as the sort of place one comes home on leave from, since it only becomes clear a few speeches later that this has, indeed, been the cause of

Walter's absence. Before this, the talk has been of the curtains that Milly says Annie should have done "the other way"; [81] of the cake that "comes from down the road"; and of the chocolate that Walter has brought for Milly—but not for Annie. "He didn't forget that I don't like chocolates," she says, proudly. [83]

This lengthy opening scene between Walter and his aunts sets a tone of normality, of bland acceptance, against which the later conflicts can be sounded. The humour is characteristic:

> ANNIE: I bet you never had a tart in prison, Wally.
> WALTER: No, I couldn't lay my hands on one. [84]

And even after the traumatic revelation that Walter's room has been let, the placatory tone of the aunts is exactly modulated to their existing relationship with Walter. So, even, are the hungover-from-childhood rebukes to which they are provoked:

> ANNIE: She's bought a lovely coverlet, she's put it on.
> WALTER: A coverlet? I could go out now, I could pick up a coverlet as good as hers. What are you talking about coverlets for?
> MILLY: Walter, don't shout at your aunt, she's deaf. [87]

The style is familiar, but not forced. And the assurance with which Pinter slots-in the short scene which follows, between Walter and Sally, before returning to the more measured pace of the living room—where Solto is having his tea with the aunts, and carrying on in a landlordly way about his tax troubles and his life story—is marred only by Walter's over-fortuitous discovery of the photograph. [92] Solto's long, rambling speeches and polite condescensions—"still on the post office books?" he asks Walter [96]—make him instantly recognisable as "the best landlord in the district" of Annie's earlier, innocent description: [82] and his agreement to look for the original of Walter's photograph is carried off with just the right air of a man who must admit to a bluff knowledge of the underworld.

The following episodes—and this is something it's easy to forget while reading the play—are all supposed to be seen from the aunts' point of view. In bed, the old pair go through a bedtime good food guide: and then Annie, hearing Walter go into Sally's room, tiptoes to the door and listens. What she hears is a mutually misleading conversation between the man and the woman, Walter playing up his criminal record for all it's worth, and trying to impress Sally with the pretence that he's a gunman, while the girl puts on her cultured face. In performance, it's important that Sally should remain very much in control—and this the watching Annie's preconceptions about the girl no doubt helps to ensure. Her response to Walter's inflated boasting graduates from polite reassurance to thinly-veiled sarcasm—she is not so very different, after all, from the girl swopping experiences with her fellow hostesses in the changing room a few scenes later.

At the night club, Solto is talking to the manager, his old acquaintance Tully, who is small-time-proprietorial about his success:

> We got a very nice clientele come in here. You know, you get a lot of musicians . . . er . . . musicians coming down here. They make up a very nice clientele. Of course, you get a certain amount of business executives. I mean, high-class people. I was talking to a few of them only the other night. They come over from Hampton Court, they come, from Twickenham, from Datchet. [107]

This, too, fits into the developing pattern of the play, for it shows Solto in his natural element—not in his landlord's hat, nor in the mature-rakish one he is about to don for Sally's benefit, but among his own kind. The following scene in the dressing-room shows Sally in similarly uninhibited circumstances, casually threatening to kick a client "in the middle of his paraphernalia one of these days". [108] Then both Sally and Solto slip the masks back into position—malleably at first, for they are new acquaintances—for their brief encounter.

Sadly, the business of tying up the plot constricts the rounding-off of these character relationships. Solto meets Walter to put him off the scent, Sally departs, and aunts and nephew resign themselves to their loss—brooding, at the last, over a photo Sally has left behind, of herself in a netball team. [114–15] This—together with Walter's peremptory and implausible ordering-about of Sally at the end of the bedroom scene [105–6]—recalls, not at all helpfully, the situation of *A Night Out*, and confirms Pinter's own feeling that at this stage he was in danger of "slipping into a formula".[37] But the most obviously formulaic element in the play is the embattled room itself. Walter's despairing reflection, "If only I could get my room back! I could get settled in, I could think, about things!" [97] is only the most clearly stated indication of his dependence upon the room, and the speech also hints at its simultaneous usefulness as a sort of scaled-down Sidcup, an excuse for putting things off.

Walter's relationship with Sally has, however, very little to do with the room. Her possession of "his" bed is a matter of sexual jealousy, not of symbolism, and although he shies away from her tentative offer of "sharing" the room, [100] Walter himself admits to Sally:

I don't know why I made such a fuss about this room. It's just an ordinary room, there's nothing to it. I mean if you weren't here. If you weren't in it, there'd be nothing to it. [105]

Whether or not Walter means this, it is my own impression of the play that the insistent motif of that pinteresque room does get unnecessarily in the way of the dramatist's developing interest in the way people adapt to one another, and in the games they play in the process of accepting or rejecting advances. In this respect, the plot of *Night School* is also distractingly dense: but its emotional patterning is clear, and —except in the last five minutes or so of the action—carefully sustained.

If *Night School* is most interesting in that it looks forward to the sexual themes of Pinter's later plays, *The Dwarfs*— first broadcast on the Third Programme in December 1960, and subsequently, unhappily, directed by Pinter himself[38] as a stage play at the Arts Theatre in 1963—is most revealing as a kind of philosophical coda to his earlier writing. As an independent work of art it is tantalisingly tangential: for the tangents are all thrown off towards Pinter's other plays. The work had its origins in an unpublished novel written during the early fifties:[39] so it's scarcely surprising that it has the allusive density of a seminal work, even though this has been transmuted, in the later dramatic process, into a retrospective progress-report. Pinter himself admits it may seem "the most intractable, impossible piece of work" to others, because only he knows "the things that aren't said, and the way the characters actually look at each other".[40] Nevertheless, I think it's well worth looking at what *is* said—although I agree that "the way the characters look" presents an almost insuperable difficulty to a stage performance.

The Dwarfs as it stands is, then, really a play for voices, and the only one of Pinter's plays to date which does shrink when it is *seen*—if one excepts *A Slight Ache* which works better on sound for the negative reason that, unseen, its tricksiness is a little less obvious. Here, an action which begins quite straightforwardly as Len and Pete visit Mark's unoccupied house "in a London suburb", [91] quickly focuses upon and is focused by the consciousness of Len himself. The subsequent action shifts between the homes of Mark and Len, Len visiting Mark or being visited by Pete: but all the while Len is drifting with increasing intensity into soliloquies about the eponymous dwarfs, little urban scavengers whose attendant Len imagines himself to be. And when Mark and Pete—whose mutual antagonism is an insistent undercurrent all through the action, each warning Len that the other is bad company for him—finally bump into one another, it turns out that Len is in hospital. There, the pair visit him, quarrel openly, and leave the play's closing speech to Len, seemingly little changed . . . or is he?

The situation is paradigmatic of *The Caretaker*. Like Aston, Len is supposed to be "looking after the place" for Mark. [92] And Pete is trying to wean him away from the dangerous friendship of Mark, as Mick is trying to separate Aston and Davies. Like Aston, Len and his friends are "in their thirties", [91] and Len's visions of the dwarfs have that hallucinatory clarity described by Aston in the earlier play:

> I used to get the feeling I could see things . . . very clearly . . . everything . . . was so clear . . . everything used to get very quiet . . . everything got very quiet . . . . all this . . . quiet . . . and . . . this clear sight . . . it was . . . but maybe I was wrong. [55]

D

I personally feel that *The Caretaker* is much more fully the "play about betrayal and distrust" that Pinter has declared *The Dwarfs* to be.[41] For *The Dwarfs* has not the objective correlative such a play almost presupposes: rather, its progress is marked by the procession of Len's fearful visions, which the commonplace comments of Pete or Mark usually puncture, as if in reality, but which they sometimes encourage and expand, as if Len is remoulding what his friends say in his own mind, so that this chimes with his own immediate sense of reality.

The dwarfs themselves are like any or all of the mysterious intruders in Pinter's earliest plays—the blind Negro of *The Room*, the Matchseller in *A Slight Ache*, Ben and Gus in *The Dumb Waiter*—but they share in particular the almost chirpy malignity of Stanley's self-appointed guardians in *The Birthday Party*. Maybe, like Len, Stanley is really being carted away to a mental home at the end of *The Birthday Party*? Strictly, the suggestion is a non-starter, because it is prompted by the back-and-forth analogising between plays that *The Dwarfs* irresistibly tempts one into, and by nothing in *The Birthday Party* as such. By the same token, however, it would be wrong to interpret *The Dwarfs* itself as if it had no independent existence, or any purpose beyond a tracing out of parallels to other plays. Certainly, it is unique in *form* among its author's works: is its content, then, self-sufficient, or merely interesting as a dramatist's report on his creative career to date?

Most critics have considered *The Dwarfs* to be a play about the impossibility of ascertaining identity, taking their cue from Len's last long speech to Pete, which begins:

The point is, who are you? Not why or how, nor even what. I can see what, perhaps, clearly enough. But who are you? It's no use saying you know who you are just because you tell me you can fit your particular key into a particular slot which will only receive your particular key because that's not foolproof and certainly not conclusive. Just because you're inclined to make these statements of faith has nothing to do with me. It's not my business. Occasionally I believe I perceive a little of what you are but that's pure accident. Pure accident on both our parts, the perceived and the perceiver. [111]

Now *The Dwarfs* is indisputably about "the perceived and the perceiver". But—except in the short, not quite climactic scene between Pete and Mark—the perceiver *throughout* the play is Len. And whilst it is dangerous to read too much into Pinter's plays, it is best not to ignore such of his hand as the dramatist *does* declare.

In this case, he declares that Len is an advanced schizophrenic—"ready for the loony bin next week", as Pete puts it [93]—from whose particular incapacity it would be utterly wrong to draw general philosophic conclusions about the human condition. Unless, of course, one believes—and there's much less evidence for this in Pinter's other works than might be thought—that the human condition consists in a permanent hovering on the brink of insanity. Pinter at his most pessimistic is not prone to such modish generalisations—indeed, to generalisations at all. Thus, it is the *particular* we must identify and understand here, as in his other plays.

Now another thing—and it's easy to forget—that Pinter is careful to particularise is *where* the action of *The Dwarfs* takes place. It is evidently important that the shifts between Mark's and Len's houses should be dramatically seen or sensed to have taken place—and that Pete is thus a visitor to them both. The opening scene takes place in Mark's

house: he has "been away longer than two weeks". [92]
It ends with his return. "A door slams. Voices of greeting.
Silence." [95] And the following sequence is immediately
located by Len's long speech defining his own domesticity.
"I have my compartment", it closes. "All is ordered, in its
place, no error has been made. I am wedged. Here is my
arrangement, and my kingdom. There are no voices. They
make no hole in my side." [96]

Mark joins him here, to be followed, separately, by Pete:
and the change of companion is itself marked by a silence,
which is broken by a remark which immediately establishes
that the location has not changed. "This is a very solid table,
isn't it?" asks Pete: and the question has its structural
importance, as well as its solipsistic.[42] [98] Len's next visit
to Mark is similarly prepared, Mark's opening instruction
"Put that mirror back," [101] at once asserting the interest
of ownership. But from this scene onwards the location
becomes more fluid in space and time, its sensory quality
increasingly shaped by Len's own consciousness, until the
abrupt change of mood during the meeting between Mark
and Pete—their first direct confrontation—when Len's
hospitalisation brings the action down to earth again.

The changing domestic settings, though carefully distinguished in the early scenes, are not, however, sustained
very fully in verbal terms: it is simply their *familiarity* which
Pinter needs to establish—of which more anon. The recurrent
imagery is of food, fresh or stale—the fortnight-old milk in
Mark's cupboard, [92] the sandwiches and the sausages Len
used to fix for himself, [94] the butter that's going up in
price, [98] the toast that he may or may not make with the
toasting-fork, [102] the tinned milk gobbled by the dwarfs,
[103] and the "rat steak" prepared by Len for the dwarfs,
but which they won't touch at first:

Where is it, they've hidden it, they're hiding it, till the time I can no longer stand upright and I fall, they'll bring it out then, grimed then, green, varnished, rigid, and eat it as a victory dish. [105]

Then there is the cause to which Len attributes his illness:

Cheese. Stale cheese. It got me in the end. I've been eating a lot of cheese. [112]

And, finally, in the play's closing speech, all the leftovers— of food, of the knacker's yard—are gathered together, only to be cleared away and a fresh start promised:

I'm left in the lurch. Not even a stale frankfurter, a slice of bacon rind, a leaf of cabbage, not even a mouldy piece of salami, like they used to sling me in the days when we told old tales by suntime. They sit, chock-full. But I smell a rat. They seem to be anticipating a rarer dish, a choicer spread.

And this change. All about me the change. The yard as I know it is littered with scraps of cat's meat, pig bollocks, tin cans, bird brains, spare parts of all the little animals, a squelching squealing carpet, all the dwarfs' leavings spittled in the muck, worms stuck in the poisoned shit heaps, the alleys a whirlpool of piss, slime, blood, and fruit juice.

Now all is bare. All is clean. All is scrubbed. There is a lawn. There is a shrub. There is a flower. [116]

And there is a stunning purity about that last couple of lines, which creates a sudden, unexpected catharsis at the climactic moment of the play.[43]

I find it impossible to define exactly why those lines are so exactly right—why the play would have been so irremediably flawed had it ended on the garbage heap of its penultimate paragraph. Indeed, as a whole *The Dwarfs* is the most impenetrable of Pinter's plays, the lilliputian yahoos of the title and of Len's visions explicable on no terms but their own. But I don't think it's too fanciful—remembering the evident care with which Pinter picks his titles—to suggest that one of the things the plays is "about" is a sense of proportion. As Pete says to Len, during his only speech of more than a few lines:

> The apprehension of experience must obviously be depen-
> dent upon discrimination if it's to be considered valuable.
> That's what you lack. You've got no idea how to preserve
> a distance between what you smell and what you think
> about it. You haven't got the faculty for making a simple
> distinction between one thing and another. Every time
> you walk out of this door you go straight over a cliff.
> What you've got to do is nourish the power of assessment.
> [99]

Martin Esslin believes that this "plea for realism" of Pete's must be qualified by the account of the dream which follows it up—and that Pete is thus as enmeshed in fantasy, for all his common-sense, as Len.[44] But Pete's dream—of being caught up in a panic in a tube station, and perceiving that everybody's skin, probably his own too, is "dropping off like lumps of cat's meat"—*is* a dream, and known to be so. It is cautionary and it is precise: cautionary in that, following as it does Pete's explicit warning to Len, it *illustrates* that the unconscious is always ready to narrow the gap between the experience and the response. And precise, therefore, *because* it is imprecise.

Ronald Hayman's suggestion[45] that the dream reflects "the fear of losing identity" is, after all, as tenable as Martin Esslin's—or as my own, that it is a fairly typical nightmare of the nuclear holocaust, deep shelters, effects of radiation and all. The particular interpretation doesn't matter: what does matter is that it *is* a dream, and that Pete can distinguish it as such. Len is fast losing the remnants of this power of discrimination—the power of identifying the gap between the experience and the response. Arguably, the loss involves not a diminishing but a heightening of sensibility, a hallucinatory sense of the immediate. Much less arguably, it also involves the loss of one's sanity.

Perhaps I am as wrong to see Pete's speech as the philosophical core of *The Dwarfs* as I believe others have been wrong in putting too much faith in Len's questioning of the nature of identity. But the fact that it is Pete's *only* pronouncement of such substance (indeed, the only set-speech in the play outside Len's stream of consciousness) tends to give it more theatrical weight. Wrong or not, it *is* in Len's failure to "preserve a distance between what you smell and what you think about it" that the poetry—and the horror—of the play lies. Instead of that distance, there are the dwarfs, acting upon and re-interpreting for Len all that is familiar in his bed-sit environment—and in particular, picking over its more grossly physical features, which become invested with the horror of a warped (or maybe just an over-developed) insight:

I squashed a tiny insect on a plate the other day. And I brushed the remains off my finger, with my finger, with my thumb. Then I saw that the fragments were growing, like fluff. As they were falling, they were becoming larger, like fluff. I had put my hand into the body of a dead bird.
[104]

The Dwarfs is impossible to simplify or to sum up: but Len's particular experience here is in one sense a microcosmic image of his condition.

Thus, in the world of *The Dwarfs*, squashing an insect on the side of a plate *is* putting a hand into the body of a dead bird. Going out of a door *is* going straight over a cliff. Hence the need for the familiar domesticity of the play's environment, and for Len to confront with sartrean nausea the everyday objects of his own home, or the known but slightly more alien objects of Mark's—the mirror, and the toasting-fork, which Len handles with such fascination or fear. [101–2] The room, which in Pinter's earliest work was a place of refuge which yet threatened betrayal, is now the preserve of the dwarfs. A few years later, the shifting surfaces of *The Dwarfs* long since scoured clean as Len's final, purified yet bleak vision prophesied, another Len might be sitting on a bed in a room he "should have been looking after" for another Mark, telling another Pete about his days among the dwarfs. But that's another story, and, as it happened, Pinter had already told it, in *The Caretaker*. Here, he is going over old ground, but with an insight shaped and made certain yet subtle by its familiarity.

4

The Love Chases

The Collection, The Lover and *The Homecoming*

SEX HAS MORE TIME to rear its several sorts of head in the posher parts of London and the stockbroker-belt of Surrey— the settings of *The Collection* and *The Lover* respectively. Pinter's only previous excursion outside the seedier urban areas, *A Slight Ache*, had been a relative failure: and in this later pair of plays, too, there is something uncertain about the ambience. This uncertainty has to do not so much with Pinter's ear for the idiom of a more cultured class as with the heightened linguistic and emotional self-consciousness of those of its members he makes his characters: so that struggles for dominance, and, in particular, acts of sexual assertion, become *mannered*—of the characters' as well as the dramatist's own accord. Human behaviour reduces itself to a sequence of chessboard manœuvres, and the plays shrink into dramatised chess problems. White to play and mate in six scenes. In *The Homecoming* this sense of abstracted cal- culation—of calculation only off-handedly connected with the players of the game—is given a more familiar, working- class background: but it becomes even less purposeful or, for that matter, interesting.

The Collection was written for television, and first screened in May 1961. But it is scripted for the stage, and requires only a single setting, split between "two peninsulas and a promontory". A telephone box is upstage centre on the promontory—a street—whilst the peninsulas accommodate Harry and Bill's house in Belgravia on one side of the stage, and James and Stella's flat in Chelsea on the other. [8] All four characters are in the rag trade—but the "collection" of the title is not simply the fashion show at which Bill and Stella may or may not have bumped into each other in Leeds a week before the play begins. The characters themselves are a "collection", too—a set of pieces in the game that is to be enacted.

The play begins on a note of vague menace: but here the vagueness and menace alike are gambits that James—making a mysterious phone-call to Bill at four o'clock in the morning, but getting Harry on the line instead—might have picked up from seeing a Pinter play, rather than a right-feeling ploy of his own. [9-10] However, the scene-setting snippets which immediately follow are much better, evoking the atmosphere in the two homes on the morning after with a minimum of verbal fuss or formal exposition. Stella is about to leave for work: her status is evidently equal if not superior to that of James in their common craft, yet she seems wistfully uncertain of her husband, who is distant, almost disinterested.

There's less doubt who is boss in Belgravia. Harry doesn't actually order Bill about, but it's clear that Bill is the maid-of-all-work around the place—his failures, whether to make toast or to mend the stair rod, irritating Harry the more for the suspicions he evidently entertains about that phone call in the small hours. Which of the two is the dominant partner in their homosexual relationship is not so certain, however, and Harry is therefore careful not to be too precise about the master–servant relationship:

I'm sick and tired of that stair-rod. Why don't you screw it in or something? You're supposed . . . you're supposed to be able to use your hands. [12]

Bill, like James, is in stay-at-home mood. "Wonderful life you lead," comments Harry: but it is evidently very much at Harry's behest—certainly socially, and no doubt sexually too. [12]

James makes a second phone call, and this time he does get Bill on the line: but he doesn't put in the threatened personal appearance until Bill has gone out (in spite of his previous intention). And so it is Harry, making the obvious connections, who opens the door to the stranger who refuses to give his name. At last, that evening, James succeeds in tracking down his quarry, and eventually, in as roundabout a way as possible, he makes his accusation: that Bill slept with his wife when they stayed in the same hotel in Leeds. At first Bill denies everything: by the end of the scene, a scene of imminent and actual threat, he seems to have admitted everything.

James proceeds vicariously to play off Stella and Bill against one another, whilst Harry becomes vicious and vituperative in his jealousy. James and Bill even strike up a seeming friendship: but this is merely the accuser engineering an opportunity to attack the accused. He does so, rather ineffectually, with a knife—watched by an unseen Harry, who makes a casual entrance to tell James that Stella has confessed "that she's made the whole thing up". [42] What Stella has really said at her brief meeting with Harry is that her husband has himself fantasised the affair: but after witnessing the verbal humiliation of Bill by Harry, who attributes his "admission" of guilt to his "slum sense of humour", [42–3] it is with the broken Bill's final, halting version of the story that James confronts his wife on his return:

> I never touched her . . . we sat . . . in the lounge, on a
> sofa . . . for two hours . . . talked . . . we talked about it
> . . . we didn't . . . move from the lounge . . . never went
> to her room . . . just talked . . . about what we would do
> . . . if we did get to her room . . . two hours . . . we never
> touched . . . we just talked about it . . . [44–5]

And as the curtain falls, Stella is just looking at James, "neither confirming nor denying" an accusation of innocence which has somehow come to seem more culpable than the earlier confession of guilt. [45]

Is Stella innocent? If so, why has she made up the story of her seduction, and why has Bill supported it? If not, why has he made up so mutually humiliating a story? And why does he try to avoid James early in the play? What private spleen is he then working off against Harry, in cultivating James with all the variant versions of the event? What version *does* James believe? And who cares? The original incident, in any of its various forms, is so trivial that it can only take on a catalytic interest in the emotional game in which the four characters get caught up. But so much dramatic importance—not to mention that climactic emphasis—is attached to *what really happened* that the irony of the "truth" (whatever it is) making, in the end, remarkably little difference is lost. And the conventions are so structured that one cannot doubt the existence of *some* objective version of that truth. What the characters say is not controlled by genuinely differing interpretations of or responses to experience, but by what effect they create—or are manœuvred into creating—upon their emotional antagonists.[46]

Pinter almost seems to be parodying his own earlier remark about the "desire for verification". As Bill asks James:

Surely the wound heals when you know the truth, doesn't it? I mean, when the truth is verified? I would have thought it did. [39]

Far too much of the action is taken up in boy-detective games of catching people out and cheating them into unwary admissions for the wilful concealment and pirandellising of the truth not to have a profound effect upon the play. Consider a couple of examples of this. Bill, questioning James about the details of love-making into which his wife's confession has gone, carefully leads him into the statement that "she scratched a little". But Bill, as he trumpingly points out, is unscarred. [21] And Harry, visiting Stella, is as crafty as some storybook private-eye at coaxing her story out of her by appearing to know it already. [34–7] The characters themselves are thus too busy trying to prove their own circumstantial cases for the audience not to be interested in the verdict—and, in this interest, to be distracted from the tensions *between* the characters, which a verifiable incident could have served to generate and not to obfuscate (just as, earlier, the resolving of any doubt as to Sally's real profession in *Night School* had allowed attention to centre fruitfully upon the series of character-opposing scenes).

What is interesting in *The Collection*, though it's hard to make out below the opaque surface, is quite another kind of ambiguity from that surrounding Bill and Stella's possible assignation—the ambiguity inherent in the different combinations of sexual attraction and repulsion which are at work. It is to further or to falsify their feelings for an individual of the opposite or the same sex that the characters interpret past actions and shape up to present events—trying to sort out those feelings for themselves and, usually, to conceal them from their object. True, Stella—torn between the habit of superficial respectability and a leaning towards sexual licence—tacks too neatly onto the procession of Pinter's actual or potential prostitutes. But her role is less central than were to be those of Sarah in *The Lover* or Ruth in *The Homecoming*; and because she herself appears sublimely unconcerned about the truth of her own tale, she is among the more successful of Pinter's many creations of her kind. She has made herself the centre of sexual attention, and—although she is distressed by James's affectation of friendship for Bill, before Harry's visit reassures her that it is all part of the sexual strategy—this is enough.

Stella's arm's-length distance from James and even her brief, sisterly mateyness towards Harry are rendered surely enough. But more interesting and better sustained is the triangular relationship between the men—Pinter's first clear study in homosexual feelings. Bill is flattered by the hint implicit in James's accusations of his own potency, and, presumably, versatility: perhaps this is why he doesn't deny the charges too strenuously. He enjoys entertaining James, and playing upon Harry's jealousy—but eventually he finds himself isolated between the two other men, the verbal onslaught of the one even more virulent than the physical violence of the other. And, Bill's humiliation completed, his torturers make civil overtures at one another until their attention can only be regained by a confession of the truth . . . or of a new lie, as the case may be.

The barely restrained fury and contempt brooding behind Harry's love-hatred for Bill makes his outburst rhetorically the most forceful passage in the play:

There's a certain kind of slum mind which is perfectly all right in a slum, but when this kind of slum mind gets out of the slum it sometimes persists, you see, it rots everything. That's what Bill is. There's something faintly putrid about him, don't you find? Like a slug. There's nothing wrong with slugs in their place, but he's a slum slug; there's nothing wrong with slum slugs in their place, but this one won't keep his place—he crawls all over the walls of nice houses, leaving slime, don't you, boy? He confirms stupid sordid little stories just to amuse himself, while everyone else has to run round in circles to get to the root of the matter and smooth the whole thing out. All he can do is sit and suck his bloody hand and decompose like the filthy putrid slum slug he is. [43]

This declaration of class warfare points to all the weaknesses and strengths of *The Collection*. Harry's remark about getting to the root of the matter is an irritating reminder that the truth-trickery is in fact unresolved, at a moment when less verifiable but dramatically more valuable truths about the characters are beginning to crystallise. The languidly logical development of Harry's indictment is completely controlled, yet cumulatively crushing rather than sequentially imaginative in its impact: and its upper-class uncouthness adds a whole new social dimension to the play. Of course, Bill's allegedly low-life origins aren't verifiable either: but his status in Harry's house is never in doubt, and neither is the effectiveness of this act of revenge.

Sadly, the stratification of social classes by speech-habits, so clear in Harry's saloon-bar abuse, isn't sustained throughout the play. Mostly, the characters talk not like members of the upper-middle class pretending to be classless, but like upper-middle class characters imitating people in plays.

"This is all rather unsubtle, don't you think?" Bill thus asks, of James's challenge to a duel with the fruit-knife. [40] The idiom is unsubtle indeed: and such truth to leisured-life as the dialogue does have only asserts that, by and large, these rag-traders are pretty boring people. That may be Pinter's intention: but whereas the boring characters of *The Birthday Party* and *Night School* were also unselfconscious, and could thus be most revealing at their most inane, in *The Collection* everybody has his tongue under control—yet neither the intellects nor the sensibilities doing the controlling prove very interesting, even in what is being concealed. Least interesting of all are those concealments which concern whether or not Bill and Stella met in Leeds, had a quick cuddle in the lift or made love all night long, or have never set eyes on one another in their lives.

The Lover, like *The Collection*, was first written for television. It was screened in March 1963, but appears in print in the version produced at the Arts a few months later. The single stage set incorporates two areas—the living room and hall downstairs, and bedroom upstairs, of Richard and Sarah's "tasteful, comfortable" house near Windsor. [49] As in *The Collection*, a wife is playing at having a lover: and once again, the husband appears to be taking it in his civilised stride. As it turns out, however, Max, the amorous afternoon caller discussed so frankly by husband and wife over their aperitifs turns out to be a kinkier *alter ego* of Richard himself. The "lovers", believing that variety is the spice of lust, evidently choose to act out impromptu rapes or seductions as the mood takes them during their matinee mating-games, and to reserve the straighter sex for their evening performances as a married couple.

But this afternoon Max starts complicating matters by saying that he can't go on deceiving his "wife", and wondering how Sarah's husband can connive at his own cuckolding. As in *The Collection*, pirandellian complications seem about to set in: and when Richard returns in his role as tired businessman in the evening, he duly demands that the lover's visits must stop. But his real intention in coming the heavy husband seems to be a wish for a new variation of role-swopping. Tired of Max's fantasy mistress, he goads his wife into pretending (and now Sarah is imitating Stella's tactics in the previous play more directly) that her fantasy lover has not been the only one:

> Do you think he's the only one who comes! Do you? Do you think he's the only one I entertain? Mmmnn? Don't be silly. I have other visitors, other visitors, all the time, I receive all the time. Other afternoons, all the time. When neither of you know, neither of you. I give them strawberries in season. With cream. Strangers, total strangers. But not to me, not while they're here. [81]

Here, however, it seems less likely that Sarah is genuinely trying to make Richard believe that she is deceiving him, than that she is tentatively feeling for the rules of the new game he is inventing. For Richard has admitted earlier:

> I haven't got a mistress. I'm very well acquainted with a whore, but I haven't got a mistress. There's a world of difference. [55]

It is evidently this world he now wants to explore—to discover "how shall I put it . . . someone who could express and engender lust with all lust's cunning. Nothing more." [57] And so Sarah slips into her new role. "You lovely whore", are Richard's last words to her in the play. Max is no longer visiting his mistress: but Richard's himself again, and visiting his whore.

The Lover is Pinter's most openly erotic work, not only in its titillating verbal love-play, but also in the various visual motifs which become charged with a sexual stimulus—notably, the bongo drums on which the husband beats out his mating-call as Max. Words and emotional mood are intimately related, and the action is, in essence, a developing emotional mood. Thus, the play is more certain of its direction than *The Collection*, and far less tied up in the entrails of its own plot. Such is the built-in economy of its characterisation, indeed, that one television critic at the time of the first production opined that it was hard on Alan Badel to have to double two major parts! Such literal-mindedness aside, all these factors enabled Pinter to restate the theme of his previous play with greater emotional clarity here, and with the ambiguities underpinning the main action instead of undermining it.

But *The Lover* shares a fault which always distinguishes a "good" minor play of Pinter's from his major work. It is anecdotal, and once one knows the punch-line of the anecdote there's not a lot of interest left. Just as the plot of *The Collection* only clarifies itself in the first scene between James and Stella, where at least a subjective basis for James's charges against Bill is established for the first time, [29–30] so it is only when Max actually keeps his afternoon assignation in *The Lover* that the business in the earlier scenes clicks into the right perspective. [63] And then it does so with all the tiresomely tied-up precision of the final chapter of a who-dunit. After one's first moment of double-take, one begins first to question the dramatic function of the audience being kept in the dark—and thus unaware of the implications of the earlier husband-wife exchanges—and secondly to feel niggling doubts about the developing sexual situation.

Half the play (not knowing what the other half is about to do) is thus about a permissive couple who are almost irritating in their bland open-mindedness. "Sounds utterly sterile", comments Sarah, of Richard's "quick cup of cocoa" relationship with his whore. [55-6] And whilst she occasionally thinks of Richard "sitting at a desk going through balance sheets and graphs" during her afternoons with Max, it "makes it all the more piquant". [53-4] Richard and his whore discuss Sarah "as we would play an antique music box. We play it for our titillation."

SARAH: I can't pretend the picture gives me great pleasure.
RICHARD: It wasn't intended to. The pleasure is mine.
SARAH: Yes, I see that, of course. [58]

As in *The Lover*, the impression is of people talking like people they have seen in pseudo-sophisticated drawing-room comedies: and there might have been both dramatic and parodistic point to this, if one *knew* that the whole thing was an elaborately shared charade anyway. But, because the whole tension and tempo of the piece depends on an audience *not* knowing this, the play quickly palls when one returns to it a second or third time. Instead of relishing one's acquired hindsight, one is merely annoyed by the little tricks of concealment.

When a play depends on the impossibility of its own verification, there is obviously no need for concealments: the question simply doesn't arise. What is declared, and no more than this, *is* the play. But where, as here, the playwright has chosen to write in his own belated verification, there is a need for complete openness with an audience if more than mere surprise is sought. Because there is no such openness here, much of interest that lies just beneath the surface of *The Lover* has less chance to divert and redirect the attention. Like Osborne's *Under Plain Cover*, the play is very much concerned with the place of fantasy in a marital relationship —indeed, with the fantasies *within* the fantasy, as Richard, playing Max, quick-changes between subsidiary roles of rapist, rescuer and the like. But the values of such sexual byplay are put to no sort of test. That the entire proceedings aren't taking place in some Windsor Castle in the air is carefully, indeed interruptively, established by the brief appearance of a very mundane milkman a few moments before Max: [62-3] but the couple's life cries out for a more fully identified context.

What is the quality of their "real" married partnership? How have the couple supported their family life during ten years of mixed double-bedmanship? Are Max's pretended children, who'll "be out of boarding school" at any moment, [71] also Richard's real ones? Is the transference of the fantasy-affair to the evening hours simply a matter of Richard getting fed up with an "eternal teatime", a "milk jug and teapot" lust? [60] Is it a febrile impromptu which gets out of hand? Or does it indeed signal some more profound reversal in the nature of the fantasy-in-progress? If so, what are its effects going to be on the reality? Such questions wouldn't even arise if Pinter had shaped the play according to more self-sufficient conventions: as it is, such doubts distract one from the *quality* of the fantasy as such, but are answered only in pirandellian side-tracking— identity-games about whether Richard is really jealous of his own *alter ego*, or Sarah of hers:

SARAH: But your wife . . . knows. Doesn't she? You've told her . . . all about us. She's known all the time.

MAX: No, she doesn't know. She thinks I know a whore, that's all. Some spare-time whore, that's all. That's what she thinks.

SARAH: Yes, but be sensible . . . my love . . . she doesn't mind, does she?

MAX: She'd mind if she knew the truth, wouldn't she?

SARAH: What truth? What are you talking about?

MAX: She'd mind if she knew that, in fact . . . I've got a full-time mistress, two or three times a week, a woman of grace, elegance, wit, imagination— [70]

As Sarah asks, what truth? Neither the quality of the language—at a pinch, all this double-talk could at least have been made comic—nor the depth of the thought, which is shallowly mandarin-maudlin, prompts one, after the surprises of a first acquaintance have been assimilated, to seek to know more or better. Maybe a certain instantaneous interest is no more than one should expect of a play written to fill a slot in a television schedule: but one had come to expect much more when the playwright concerned was Harold Pinter.

The Lover was followed, after an interval of two years, by *Tea Party* on television and *The Homecoming* on the stage— the productions taking place within a couple of months of one another. And Pinter's admirers at this time either began to feel, as I did myself, that the dramatist was writing himself out, or, with John Russell Taylor, that "a new, 'objective' phase" in his work was opening.[47] We were both wrong. *The Homecoming* proved to be the final experiment in what was actually Pinter's second "objective" phase. And *Tea Party*, like *The Basement* (which was written at about this time, though not performed till 1967), in fact marked a transition between one mode of writing and another, and was not, as I had feared, merely a symptom of fragmentation foreshadowing the final breakdown of the brand of formalised realism which Pinter had employed in *The Homecoming*. Because of this, I'm juggling slightly with the strict chronological sequence of the plays in this section. For *The Homecoming* clearly belongs among the semi-realistic love chases, whilst *Tea Party* holds promise of the better things that were to come.

The Homecoming, then, opened at the Aldwych in June 1965, to considerable critical acclaim. And Pinter himself, in the interview he gave rather over a year later, was evidently pleased with its achievement:

> The only play which gets remotely near to a structural entity which satisfies me is *The Homecoming*. *The Birthday Party* and *The Caretaker* have too much writing . . . I want to iron it down, eliminate things.[48]

Now if that was truly Pinter's instinct at this stage of his career, the earlier full-length plays he here deprecates show how wise he had been not to have given it free rein before: surely, *The Homecoming* is its *reductio ad absurdum*. His more recent work has, indeed, shown how "eliminating things" can—given a more appropriate *formal* vehicle—contribute to the shaping of a "structural entity". But in *The Homecoming* the dissociation between form and content is absolute, and one is left incredulous at the aimlessness of plot and arbitrariness of feeling alike.

At the play's centre of gravity is Ruth, wife of the brain-drained college professor Teddy, whose "homecoming" after six years' absence gives the play its title. His father Max, his bachelor uncle Sam, and two younger brothers Lenny and Joey—a professional ponce and a building-labourer-cum-boxer respectively—are still living in the "old house in

North London" [6] where Teddy's own youth was spent. They greet the return of this prestigious prodigal with a mixture of open hostility, sentimental gush, and, as far as Ruth is concerned, suspicion tinged with sexual envy. There are moments of raw violence, but most of the play consists in circuitous talk—recriminations about the past and inane quarrels about the present, plus an admixture of cross-purposed dialogue about trivialities.

The sum total of the talk is a raked-up revelation about an incident long buried in the past—the revelation prompted by the imminent repetition of such an incident in the present. Apparently Max's long-dead wife Jessie, alternately eulogised and vilified throughout the play, once betrayed him with his best friend MacGregor in the back of a car driven by Sam, then as now a chauffeur by trade. Sam has a fit—or dies, nobody knows or seems to care—as soon as his secret has been unbosomed. But it seems that Ruth, like Jessie, is one of nature's tarts, and Teddy, like Sam, one of the watchers on life's sidelines. Finding out, as they think, that Ruth is an easy lay, the family try to intimidate or cajole her into remaining with them, for their pleasure and profit: and as her husband prepares to leave for the airport en route for a return to the States, Ruth, sure enough, is planning her future in the family circle he is leaving behind. Far from being coerced into prostitution, however, she remains perfectly in control of herself, and, increasingly, of the family. The homecoming is hers, too.

As a scenario, this is neither more nor less viable than *The Birthday Party*'s. But because the characterisation is, at least superficially, as realistic as *The Caretaker*'s and the dialogue as scrupulously colloquial, the problem posed by the implausibility of *what actually happens* is very much harder to overcome. Teddy and Ruth are an educated couple with three children, only slightly less self-assured in their apparent sophistication than the characters of *The Collection* or *The Lover*: and for them to have got caught up in a sort of ibsen-esque heredity-rite, in a play which itself crashes through the gears from the realistic to the ritualistic as if a learner-dramatist were in the driving-seat, is hard enough to take. That Pinter lapses in *The Homecoming* into limitations he had seemingly long ago transcended is harder—and sadder—still.

The play even has trouble over its exposition, a matter which had never before bothered Pinter in the least:

> SAM: After all, I'm experienced. I was driving a dust cart at the age of nineteen. Then I was in long-distance haulage. I had ten years as a taxi-driver and I've had five as a private chauffeur.
> MAX: It's funny you never got married, isn't it? A man with all your gifts. [14–15]

Max's response is just about excusable, as the kind of heavily ironical brick he is prone to heave now and again at his probably homosexual brother. But Sam's own potted bio-graphy, although it fits in with his tendency to utter ponder-ous and needlessly precise details about his trivial round, takes this tendency to a purely functional excess, throwing into relief how superficially character and language have been integrated in the play. Indeed, Sam is seldom much more than a structural convenience, whether as a suitably passive eye-witness of Jessie's infidelity, or in his habit—just about his *only* distinguishing characteristic—of reminis-cing more reliably than the others:

> SAM: I want to make something clear about Jessie, Max. When I took her out in the cab, round the town, I was

taking care of her, for you. I was looking after her for you,
when you were busy, wasn't I? I was showing her the
West End.
Pause.
You wouldn't have trusted any of your other brothers.
You woudn't have trusted Mac, would you? But you
trusted me. I want to remind you.
Pause.
Old Mac died a few years ago, didn't he? Isn't he dead?
Pause.
He was a lousy stinking rotten loudmouth. A bastard
uncouth sodding runt. Mind you, he was a good friend
of yours. [19]

The speech—aside from its expository clumsiness—serves
its purpose of arousing the suspicions it was intended to sooth:
of planting the seed that withers into Sam's dying speech.
But its final contradiction isn't even in Sam's easy-going
character: it's in Max's—or maybe, just in the play's
pervasive verbal mode, of creating shock-effects that signify
nothing.

The earliest speech in the play so trade-marked is this
recollection of Max's, during the first, static scene of cuss
and counter-cuss between Max and Lenny:

He was very fond of your mother, Mac was. Very fond.
He always had a good word for her.
Pause.
Mind you, she wasn't such a bad woman. Even though it
made me sick just to look at her rotten stinking face, she
wasn't such a bad bitch. I gave her the best bleeding
years of my life, anyway. [9]

And this in turn has been prepared for by the sudden change of subject that first introduces MacGregor:

> I used to knock about with a man called MacGregor. I called him Mac. You remember Mac? Eh? [9]

Returning to the play knowing just how fond Mac was of Jessie doesn't heighten one's sense of irony here: it makes it seem all the more manufactured and obvious. But at least in Max's case the speech mannerisms and motifs—the meaningless adjectival expletives, the ubiquitous use of the word "bitch" for men and women, friends and foes alike—do begin to make the man.

Because so little *happens*, and because what does happen occurs so suddenly, it's very tempting to start searching for the symbolic explanations: to find, perhaps, as one critic has done, Max's use of the word "bitch" suggestive of the "sexually chaotic situation" of the play, in which a father has been forced into the mothering role, until, at last, the whore Ruth can take over from the departed whore Jessie.[49] And the cyclical structuring of events does make such an interpretation viable—the mother, prostituting herself while Sam sat silently in attendance, now supplanted by the one-time "model" Ruth, [57] her husband standing impassively by. But it is precisely because this is essentially a *theatrical* image —Teddy's silence makes it so—that the symbolism breaks down. Teddy is *there*, his presence on a stage the more forcefully felt for his virtual speechlessness—and it is his mute but manifest presence that makes any simple, symbolic interpretation of the written words irrelevant. The mother-made-whore has not only returned as the whore-made-mother: she has been taken away from her husband, apparently with his full approval and consent. "Don't become a stranger", are her parting words to him. [81] They create some sort of *effect*, a tugging at vague emotional tripwires, as does so much of the play, in a vacuum: considered in context, they are meaningless, an over-facile farewell to enable Teddy to slip off as inconspicuously as possible.

Similarly, Sam's sudden explosion into speech, "in one breath",

MacGregor had Jessie in the back of my cab as I drove them along. [79]

is, judged as an isolated, interjected theatrical effect, fine and forceful—given the suspension of a certain kind of disbelief. But in the shaping-up of the scene, it only seems to happen because Pinter has spun out as long as he can the interest of the negotiations—themselves entrapping and a little tedious in their detail—between Ruth and Lenny over her conditions of employment, and now wants something to divert his audience's attention, and prompt a switch in subject. *The Homecoming* piles effect upon effect in a way that is reminiscent of vintage melodrama; and it demands rather the same kind of conditioned but extremely limited response. It is full of pavlovian dramatic devices, which trigger off an audience's instinctive reactions so as to induce, as required, a sense of menace, of sexual reconnoitring, or just of some ill-defined "significance". [50]

Not that Pinter would wish his play to assert any significance beyond itself—yet the only clue to what might have given it coherence and significance *within* itself, spelt out with unwonted explicitness in this speech of Ruth's, is more tantalising for the kind of play it promises than the play it is supposed to predicate:

Look at me. I . . . move my leg. That's all it is. But I wear
. . . underwear . . . which moves with me . . . it captures
your attention. Perhaps you misinterpret. The action is
simple. It's a leg . . . moving. My lips move. Why don't
you restrict . . . your observations to that? Perhaps the
fact that they move is more significant . . . than the words
which come through them. You must bear that . . . possibility . . . in mind. [52–3]

What is one to make of this? Again, as an isolative, attention-
distracting stunner it is fine: it surrounds Ruth with an aura
of smooth, soothing sexuality—and it also *changes the subject*
after Lenny has threatened to bog the action down in one
of his attempts to taunt Teddy into swopping quasi-
philosophical speculation.

Here, he has been pondering the old solipsistic favourite
about the nature and solidity of a table:

LENNY: Take a table, take it. All right, I say, *take* it, *take*
a table, but once you've taken it, what you going to do
with it? Once you've got hold of it, where you going to
take it?
MAX: You'd probably sell it.
LENNY: You wouldn't get much for it.
JOEY: Chop it up for firewood. [52]

Now one critic has solemnly argued that this dispute signals
Lenny's impotence (he *takes* the table but doesn't know what
to do with it), Max's mercenary-mindedness, and Joey's
castration complex—after all, he "didn't get all the way" in
his adventure upstairs with Ruth. [66] Her interruption of
the sterile argument could well, one feels, be Pinter crying
out to such critics. For Ruth seems to be imploring her

listeners not to try to complicate or simplify—not to *rationalise* in any manner at all: and the speech stands, washed by a slowly ebbing wave of silence, as a statement of her own quintessence and of the play's methodology. And yet, isn't it as blatant a simplification, derived from as banal a metaphysic, as those it is refuting? Ruth is using words—a carefully, compellingly poised self-definition—to deny the relevance of words. The movement of her lips is more significant than what she is saying: and yet this *is* what she is saying. *The Homecoming* certainly works best (perhaps can only work at all) as a kind of sexual mime with accompanying word-music: but words are *not* music, and their meaning, or lack of meaning, modifies the action and one's own response to it—most notably, in this very speech of Ruth's.

The speech is pivotal not only to the philosophic rationale of the play, but to the characterisation of Ruth. It is from this moment that Ruth's reversion to her origins becomes irrevocable. Before, she has been perfectly in control of herself and of those who attempt to terrorise her, at an intellectual rather than an instinctive level. Her first meeting with Lenny (though *why* it takes the offhand shape it does, as if these two total strangers were picking up the threads of an earlier acquaintance, is never at all clear) shows how consummately well she can *use* words when she wishes— whether the words are her own or, by holding her peace, she is letting Lenny lose himself in a verbal maze of his own making. Lenny's conversational style is similar to Mick's in *The Caretaker*—a confusion of carefully misplaced connectives—but his opponent has her own, more economic method of verbal warfare. Calling Lenny's bluff, by neither encouraging nor quite repelling his sexual advances, Ruth forces him into long, rambling anecdotes which put off the moment when a gesture must be made, a gambit followed through:

and so Lenny launches into a long story about a girl who began "taking liberties with me", but who was "falling apart with the pox", [31] and next into a tale about an old lady who wanted his help moving a mangle. [32–3]

Both anecdotes end in acts of violence—towards, that is, the whore of the first story, and the mother-figure of the second. Ruth takes no notice of the aggression thus harmlessly sublimated, and deigns to join in the verbal fisticuffs only when Lenny stops feinting and threatens a direct attack. He wants to take away a glass of water he has earlier brought her, an act of taking as purposeless as the gesture of giving:

> RUTH: I haven't quite finished.
> LENNY: You've consumed quite enough, in my opinion.
> RUTH: No, I haven't.
> LENNY: Quite sufficient, in my own opinion.
> RUTH: Not in mine, Leonard.
> *Pause.*
> LENNY: Don't call me that, please.
> RUTH: Why not?
> LENNY: That's the name my mother gave me.
> *Pause.*
> Just give me the glass.
> RUTH: No.
> *Pause.*
> LENNY: I'll take it, then.
> RUTH: If you take the glass . . . I'll take you. [34]

Lenny blusters on for a bit, but he is now clearly on the defensive. Ruth's superiority and sexuality are established. But at what cost? One responds to Ruth's triumph with a reflex-action of admiration: but it is for a dramatist's manipulative skill, not a woman's wiles. Ruth's temper and her tactics are alike unmotivated: their effect comes before their cause. As one so often feels in *The Homecoming*, the writing is becoming automatic—even that familiar pinteresque device of the rejected name being pressed into service to anticipate the future role of Ruth as whore and mother-figure.

Lenny's first move of all against Ruth has actually reverted to the slight-ache motif—a tick in his bedroom that's been keeping him awake.

> I mean there are lots of things which tick in the night, don't you find that? All sorts of objects, which, in the day, you wouldn't call anything else but commonplace. They give you no trouble. But in the night any given one of a number of them is liable to start letting out a bit of tick. [29]

Now this tale of a tick, and the dramatic purpose underlying it, has become, for me at least, so recognisably a pinteresque tic—here, just about halfway between Mick's purposive nonsense, and the earlier Len's sense of the threateningly inanimate in *The Dwarfs*—that it sets off a different sort of slight ache altogether: a nagging doubt, which increases as the play proceeds, that Pinter's purely technical expertise has taken over, and made such theatrical interest as remains a matter of imposing a formula upon a form.

However, at least the ineffably physical Ruth will have served some purpose if she remains a final, definitive version of all her prototype-sisters. Lulu in *The Birthday Party* was her relatively harmless, even homely embryo. The girl who picked up poor Albert in *A Night Out* was one of the less overweening members of the sorority, sheltering behind her protective pretence of a past as a continuity girl and a present as the refined mother of a girl at boarding school. Sally in

Night School, on the other hand, was doing very nicely in her chosen line, adopting her schoolteaching disguise merely for the convenience of renting her digs. These were the respectable-minded whores: but Flora in *A Slight Ache*, Stella in *The Collection* and Sarah in *The Lover* had their respectability for real, and for them it was only the symbolic, actual or fantasised taking of a lover that could create that sense of their own wholeness which Pinter's younger and sexier women have always felt to be dependent upon their sustaining the dual roles of wife and whore. Ruth is at once daughter to them all, and mother-superior to their high-class bawdy house.

This sense of the duality of the female psyche has been one of Pinter's least productive preoccupations; but here it is at least purged by being taken to excess. Ruth thus becomes even less malleable *on stage* than any of Pinter's earlier amateur or professional prostitutes—partly because here the prostitution is pivotal, partly because Ruth does have an inkling of an individual identity, which might have been developed and felt more fully had it not been overlaid by her representative role. For her, one begins to sense, living and being is an end in itself, and the immediacy of experience is all that matters. Her actions have significance in what they embody, not in what they signify—just as she claims that her words matter only because her lips are in movement. There's nothing very original about this simplified form of existential coming-to-terms with oneself, but it might have made Ruth less of a ready-made character. As it is, her existence *cannot* precede her essence: because as the *quintessence* of pinteresque womanhood, her freedom of action is hemmed in by her dramatic heredity.

In particular, this causes her change-of-heart at the peripetea of the action to seem sudden and lacking in conviction, unbalancing the whole play. Her scene alone with Teddy, during which this change first becomes perceptible, is stilted and uncomfortable—and whereas she had before been perfectly aware of Lenny's fantasising about how he would "probably have gone through Venice" if he'd been old enough to fight in the Italian campaign, [30] and although she had then gauged its sexually off-putting purpose and made use of it, now she truckles to the empty fantasy, and even feebly joins in.

> TEDDY: You liked Venice, didn't you? It was lovely, wasn't it? You had a good week. I mean . . . I took you there. I can speak Italian.
> RUTH: But if I'd been a nurse in the Italian campaign I would have been there before. [55]

This is terribly, quite tangibly wrong: it should be, almost, a moment of epiphany for Ruth, but the quality of the transmitted experience is bathetic. She "closes her eyes" as Teddy departs. Lenny appears, and she indulges in a remembrance of her modelling past—much more rhapsodic, this, but as directionless and somehow *padded* as before, so that Teddy has to return with the suitcases to generate renewed activity.

Ruth dances with Lenny, kisses him, and lapses off-handedly into a sort of mini-orgy with the two brothers, Joey embracing and Lenny caressing her inert body—whilst Max simultaneously swops friendly commonplaces with Teddy. Tremendously difficult to stage, the episode is gratuitously sensual yet strangely sexless—as ostensibly abandoned as Max's sudden outburst of violence at the end of the first act, yet so arbitrary and empty of emotion as to be almost abstract in its quality. And least of all does the scene show Ruth living in the movement of her body: like

E

the half-time whore she is, she is as impassive in a man's
embrace as her husband is in observing it.

Thus, while Max is laying about Joey and Sam, and again
while Ruth is laying about with Joey and Lenny, Teddy
stands, regarding and regardless, a lump of stage suet. What
is Teddy? An embodiment of impotent liberal humanism?
Or the foredoomed poor fish of the family? Or just the intellectual academic incapable of action? He, like Ruth, gets a
self-explanatory speech, and one draws upon it in desperation:

There's no point in my sending you my works. You'd be
lost. It's nothing to do with the question of intelligence.
It's a way of being able to look at the world. It's a question
of how far you can operate on things and not in things.
I mean it's a question of your capacity to ally the two, to
relate the two, to balance the two. To see, to be able to
see! I'm the one who can see. That's why I can write my
critical works. Might do you good . . . have a look at
them . . . see how certain people can view . . . things . . .
how certain people can maintain . . . intellectual equilibrium. Intellectual equilibrium. You're just objects. You
just . . . move about. I can observe it. I can see what you
do. It's the same as I do. But you're lost in it. You won't
get me being . . . I won't be lost in it. [62]

So there it is—Teddy's *apologia pro inertia sua*, and very
grateful one must be for it. Indeed, had the play been a kind
of clinical observation from this non-participant's point-of-
view, cinematically angled and fined-down, it might have
made more sense. But as a work for the stage, in which an
audience sees the whole family miniaturised, and through a
fixed, far-off focus, in their disproportionately huge house,
Teddy shrinks into the most dwarf-like of them all.

It's just as possible, for that matter, to fit this eldest son into the pattern of the play by thinking of him as a sort of contemporised Oedipus, who's been sleeping with his mother-substitute but loses her to the father he hasn't got the guts to kill. The trouble is that this is just one of a multitude of possible interpretations—and the number of possibilities derives not from a density to be profitably yet never definitively disentangled, but from a yawning probability gap to be filled in as best it can.

True, Teddy—holding up his intellectual equilibrium, no doubt—tells Ruth that he "can manage very easily at home ... until you come back", [76] but the play, unlike Pinter's richest and most rewarding works, fades out of existence after its final curtain. It is full of ambiguous episodes which are there rather to fill out than to enrich the action—the business of Teddy's quite out-of-character theft of Lenny's cheese-roll, [63–5] for example, or of Sam's *tête-à-tête* with his nephew, during which he confides that Teddy was "always the main object" of his mother's love. [62–3] More pervasively, the point of Uncle Sam's involvement in the action remains a mystery. He certainly provides some welcome moments of light relief with his elaborate discourses on the art of being a good chauffeur, [13–16] or with his compulsive routine of washing-up that so infuriates Max. [38–40] But as soon as Sam starts getting significant, he is either inexplicable—as at the moment of his collapse—or all too explicable, as in his function as the Teddy of an earlier generation, unable to escape the family clutches.

Max even anticipates Sam's providing for the household's sexual needs as Teddy is about to do:

When you find the right girl, Sam, let your family know, don't forget, we'll give you a number one send-off, I

promise you. You can bring her to live here, she can keep
us all happy. We'd take it in turns to give her a walk
round the park. [16]

But the dramatic irony is worse-concealed even than the
threat—and is piled on thicker still a few exchanges later,
when Max tells his family to go "and find yourself a mother".
[17] In any case, when Sam's big moment arrives nobody
seems to care a damn, either for confession or confessor.
Max, by all accounts, has never doubted that his wife was a
whore, whether or not with MacGregor: but Jessie, in spite
of his incessant passing references to her, no more comes alive
than her latter-day counterpart.

Neither, for that matter, does Max. He is a sort of instant
character, easily etched in by the violence of his language
—which consists largely in readily-rung changes on his
repertoire of curses—and by his totally erratic behaviour:
but he is never purposeful, even in his inconsistency. His role
gets considerable dramatic emphasis—it is with an impression
of Max that the play both begins and ends. Yet his opening
scene is one part exposition to two parts compinterised
characterisation, and his grand climacteric is one of the
uneasiest scenes in a play full of uneasy scenes, as, falling on
his knees, whimpering and moaning, he crawls past the
prone body of his brother, and approaches Ruth:

I'm not an old man.
  He looks up at her.
Do you hear me?
  He raises his face to her.
Kiss me.
  *She continues to touch Joey's head, lightly. Lenny stands,
  watching.* [83]

And the curtain falls. Again, the sheer grotesqueness of it all engages the attention—but only instantaneously, and without *connecting* the scene to what has gone before, let alone to any conceivable emotional reality outside the play itself. In between times, Max has merely been benevolent or bellicose, affectionate or aggressive, clever or thick-headed—yet always, one senses, as it suits Pinter's purpose, not Max's mood.

The play's shocks are thus almost exclusively the cheap thrills of non-recognition. Consider more closely Ruth's sudden inversion of Lenny's threat, already quoted—"If you take the glass . . . I'll take you." [34] The retort is neat, nicely balanced verbally, and it makes a good theatrical moment. Yet it could as well be Flora talking to the Match-seller for all its contextual relevance or particularity.[51] Similarly, Max's tale of his knack of handling racehorses might have been spun by any one of half-a-dozen of Pinter's earlier characters, and been more relevant and insightful than it is here. [10] During Lenny's rebuke of Teddy over the cheese-roll incident comes, however, the most disturbing example in the play of Pinter's loss of touch, and groping for a gratuitous laugh—a thing he has very rarely had to resort to, so surely does he usually let the laughs arise easily and incidentally out of what a character can't help but say anyway.

> Dad's getting on now, he's not as young as he used to be, but the thought of three cheeky kids looking up and calling him Grandad is probably the greatest pleasure he's got left before he dies. In fact it'll probably kill him. [65]

This is pushing things just a bit too far—a straining after effect that one notices again and again in the play, because it is little else *but* a succession of isolated effects.

The Homecoming is, in short, a modishly intellectualised melodrama, its violence modulated by its vagueness, its emotional stereotyping disguised by carefully planted oddities of juxtaposition and expression. To suspend disbelief in this play is to call a temporary halt to one's humanity. Pinter had written other bad plays, and had got fixated by his own bad habits before this: but *The Homecoming* is his only work by which I have felt myself actually soiled and diminished.[52] If a work is pornographic because it toys with the most easily manipulated human emotions—those of sex and (more especially) violence—without pausing to relate cause and effect, then *The Homecoming* can even be said to fall into such a category. One has only to think of such a roughly con- temporary work as Edward Bond's *Saved* to realise that what may be pornographically objectionable depends not on the number of blows struck, curses cursed or girls propositioned per page—because for Bond's characters even at their most callous one can feel compassion, and sense human causality. For the characters of *The Homecoming* I, at least, can feel nothing, other than an occasional shock of surprise or disgust: and even these shocks are subject to a law of rapidly dimin- ishing returns. Here, Pinter's enterprise is sick, and each thing melts in mere, unmotivated oppugnancy.

5

Passing Acquaintances

Tea Party, The Basement, Landscape,
Night, Silence and *Old Times*

EVERYMAN is an island, and if a stranger is occasionally cast up on the shore, it will only be to seek some means of retreat to a private world, more or less far away. In Pinter's latest group of plays, he measures some of the distances which isolate human beings from one another. *Tea Party* and *The Basement* are studies in loneliness and brief together-ness which create their impressions largely by the technical means Pinter had at his disposal—though had not previously felt disposed to use to the full—in using the medium of television: whilst the four short but wholly perfect stage plays rely more fully than he had ever done before on the pure interplay of words.

The television pieces are more fluid in their movement through space and time than anything else Pinter has written, whilst the stage plays are his most static. In the earlier pair he is still preoccupied with struggles for sexual possession such as had filled out the main themes of *The Collection*, *The Lover* and *The Homecoming*: but in the later works, sex has become only a single element, inseparable though it is from the broader, more retrospective vision of humankind these pieces share. So different in these several ways, all the works in this group leave one with an impression of fragmentation, controlled and made endurable by being given formal shape—and, unexpectedly, an increasingly distinct sense of *location*, whether this be evoked by the camera and telecine sequence, or merely by a memory suffused with a perception of place.

Tea Party was first produced—or, more precisely, simultaneously screened, by the sixteen member nations of the European Broadcasting Union—shortly before the opening of *The Homecoming*, in March 1965. It has since been staged, not very satisfactorily, in a double-bill with *The Basement*: and Pinter himself, describing the play as "actually a film, cinematic", continued revealingly,

> Television and films are simpler than the theatre—if you get tired of a scene you just drop it and go on to another one. (I'm exaggerating, of course.) What *is* so different about the stage is that you're just *there*, stuck—there are your characters stuck on the stage, you've got to live with them and deal with them.[53]

Hence, no doubt, the difference between *Tea Party* and *Landscape* or *Silence*—in which the characters are, inexorably, "just *there*, stuck". And perhaps there is, indeed, occasionally a feeling in *Tea Party* that Pinter *has* started to "get tired of a scene" and dropped it—though never without making its point, and thus justifying it dramatically. But on the whole the scenic variety and constant cross-cutting in the play is purposeful for what it does, not merely for what it is. *Tea Party* and *The Basement* are, in consequence, the only television or radio plays of Pinter's that do not easily adapt to live theatrical performance: for not only is the *way* the characters themselves see things so important as to rule out much simplification in the settings, but, in *Tea Party* at least, the way the central character *fails* to see things can only satisfactorily be captured by the use of the television camera, standing in for one man's failing vision.

This man is Disson, boss of a firm which manufactures sanitary ware, and proud of it. He is first seen interviewing a new personal secretary, Wendy, who tells him that she has left her previous job because her chief wouldn't "call a halt to his attentions". [11] In the course of their conversation, Disson mentions that he is getting married the next day: and in the following scenes we meet his fiancée Diana, and her brother Willy—who, owing to the illness of Disson's "oldest friend" Disley, agrees to stand in as best man. At the reception, therefore, it is Willy who proposes the toasts both to Diana and her husband: and he does so with a suavity which so impresses Disson that he invites him, apparently on the spur of the moment, to come into his business. A brief honeymoon snippet is followed by a succession of domestic cameos—Disson at his workbench, Disson and Diana at breakfast, Disson getting irritable with the twin children of his previous marriage. And this irritation is the first hint that something is not quite right: from this time on, Disson's life begins to disintegrate.

Diana, against her husband's inclination, becomes Willy's secretary. And Disson begins to feel indefinably persecuted. Like Edward, he has also developed a slight ache in his eyes —though Diana tells him that hers had "been shining for months" after their marriage [17]—and his sight at last begins playing serious tricks. Thus, he sees two ping-pong balls instead of one bouncing off the table towards him, [24] or has to make three attempts before he succeeds in tying his tie. [27] His friend Disley, who is an optician, can find nothing wrong with his eyesight: but its failures are evidently symptoms of something more than a physical malaise—a dissociation from reality, in short, in which the real or imagined plottings of Willy and Diana, the superciliousness of the twins, and the mildly kinky flirtatiousness of Wendy are compounded as evidence against his sanity.

Disson begins to depend on a particular chiffon scarf of Wendy's to protect his eyes from their failures or warpings of perception: and finally he demands to be bandaged into blindness by Disley—"my eye consultant" [46]—in which condition he sits, apparently unseeing and silent, as the tea party of the title assembles in his office. The party is to celebrate Disson's first year of marriage with Diana: and here, shots of the small-talking guests—who include Disson's elderly parents, and Disley and his prattling wife Lois, besides Wendy and all the other members of his family— crosscut with the imagined goings-on as the blindfolded Disson hallucinates them. Finally, Disson "sees" a sort of simultaneous rape by Willy of Diana and Wendy, and he falls to the floor in his chair. He is, by all appearances —which now revert to the objective for the last time— paralytically insane.

This, of course, is the second of Pinter's eponymous parties which have culminated in a spiritual and physical collapse of the supposed guest of honour. And the play has several other affinities with *The Birthday Party*. Here, too, a pair of outsiders intrude into a man's inner sanctum—which in Disson's case implicates Diana and Willy in an invasion of Disson's office as well as his home. Here, too, the victim is, symbolically or actually, blinded—Disson by a bandage, Stanley by having his spectacles broken. Here, too, is a single friend, half-sensing what is happening, who just might be able to help: but Disley turns out to be no more the best man in Disson's life than in his marriage, failing even to understand the real nature of his "unreliable" vision. [26]

Again, there is no clear reason *why* Disson is thus being victimised, or has made a victim of himself. But *The Birthday Party* did achieve something that *Tea Party* lacks—a consistently satisfying internal logic. Between Disson's feeling that the whole world is conspiring against him and one's objective glimpses of his life at home and in the office there is, until the final scene, only the narrowest of gaps: and one is therefore forced into considering, unhelpfully it seems to me, whether he is or is not the victim of a "real" conspiracy after all.

Thus, there is too much mystification for its own sake—in the menacing precociousness of the twin boys, for example, who, along with their new stepmother, even exhibit a tendency towards semantic quibbling like a pair of budding Bens and Guses. [21] That Willy and Diana are indulging in some private plotting of their own seems more consistent with their characters, but not with the character of the play: there's not space or time enough for the action to expand so as to embrace both Disson's breakdown, and, somewhere on the periphery of the play, the actual and devious goings-on between Willy and Diana which might or might not be contributory to it. One could almost believe better in Disson's increasing suspicions of the brother and sister if his foundation for them did not seem so undeniably strong.

Philosophically, the play works by systematically breaking down its victim's calm assumption of his sympathetic understanding for others. And this premise is clearly stated in what amounts to Disson's declaration of faith to his recently ensconced brother-in-law:

A man's job is to assess his powers coolly and correctly and equally the powers of others. Having done this, he can proceed to establish a balanced and reasonable

relationship with his fellows. In my view living is a matter
of active and willing participation. So is work . . . Now,
dependence isn't a word I would use lightly, but I will use
it and I don't regard it as a weakness. To understand the
meaning of the term dependence is to understand that
one's powers are limited and that to live with others is not
only sensible but the only way work can be done and dig-
nity achieved. Nothing is more sterile or lamentable than
the man content to live within himself. [19]

The action which follows is an exemplary yet cautionary
illustration of this statement, making it less a self-definition
than a self-indictment: but the speech does virtually nothing
in the way of tracing how or why Disson has taken so different
a direction from his credo. Maybe the point is, quite simply,
that involvement or estrangement are not matters of good
or bad intentions. Yet consider how the estranged Disson
contrasts with such other alienated characters of contemporary drama as Pinter's own Stanley in *The Birthday
Party*—his only instinctive self-knowledge his need for the
seeming security of Meg's lodgings—or Bill Maitland, in
Osborne's *Inadmissible Evidence*, who knows all too well that,
as an individual, he is falling apart.

Disson, unlike either, desperately keeps up appearances
until his consciousness finally parts company even from
appearances: and the inanities continue over the teacups
all around him. What he has done, or what has been done
to him, is uncertain: but Disson himself, possessing the self-
awareness that Stanley lacks, ought surely to know no less
well than Maitland the nature of his condition, albeit not
the cure for it. Yet even in Disson's attempts to avoid facing
up to the truth, one is uncertain whether the evasiveness is
intended mainly to deceive himself or others.

More interesting, however, than Disson's attempts to save face with his secretary, wife and brother-in-law, or than such side-issues as Willy's enigmatic relationship with his sister, are Disson's own fumbling attempts to achieve sexual rapport with the three women in the play. Disley's wife Lois is the least seen, yet even she, of the whimsical gushing over her bird-bath [26] and the travel-brochure mentality, [49-50] makes a slight but discernible dent upon Disson's consciousness. Wendy is more distracting, and sets out to be more of a distraction, from the beginning—her elaborate leg-crossing ritual, and her tales of being "touched" by her previous boss, [9-12] foreshadowing Disson's own fascination with the friction of her limbs upon the leather of his desk, which is indulged in the chair-climbing episode [22-3] and in his own, tentatively seductive gestures of "touching" the girl while she copes with a telephone call. [31-2] Willy seemingly outplays his brother-in-law here too, however, when he asks if he can "borrow" the girl's "services" for five minutes. Disson hears "giggles, hissing, gurgles, squeals", from the adjoining office, and tries to see what is going on at the keyhole—only to be surprised, ungainly on his knees, by the entrance of Diana from Willy's office. [33] But is the giggling for real? Or is the allegedly absent Diana's appearance no more than impressionistic confirmation of the sexual interchangeability of wife and secretary, which culminates in the imagined double-seduction at the close of the play?

Most of the crucial moments in Disson's decline are impossible to capture on a stage—his compulsive fascination with Wendy's buttocks, for example, which appear in "enormous close-up" as they swamp his own vision. [34-5] And Disson's unusually acute perception of certain colours, textures, or sensory impressions—the stain on Disley's cheek, [25] the compulsively clutched ping-pong ball [51]—cannot be adequately rendered without the intensifying aid of the camera (or, alternatively, by means of some form of narrative intervention, but this Pinter has never chosen to employ.)[54] The game of office football, with a round table-lighter Disson has knocked on to the floor, does draw back the camera for a while, however, and the symbolically sexual contest is reminiscent of the bongo-drums episodes in *The Lover* in its undeclared eroticism. But Disson declines Wendy's invitation to "tackle me", sinking helplessly to the floor: and in the following scene, in bed with Diana, she too, hints at sexual failures, suggesting that he has been "a little subdued . . . lately". [35–6]

Thus, it seems that Disson's physical potency as well as his mental stability is being drained away—so that, in the subsequent encounters with his secretary, Wendy treats him more like a well-trained pet than a potential bedfellow, appearing to satisfy some sensual need of her own in Disson's dependence upon her chiffon scarf to blank out his deceptive vision:

I always feel like kissing you when you've got that on round your eyes. Do you know that? Because you're all in the dark. [45]

Wendy here reminds one of Flora, preparing to mother the Matchseller in *A Slight Ache*. And Disson, by the end of the play, has become a reluctant version of Teddy in *The Homecoming*, incapable of movement as he watches the supposed seduction of his women. Yet what makes *Tea Party* for all its faults—which are arguably the consequences of Pinter's trying to squeeze a quart into a pint plot—so much more satisfactory a play than either *A Slight Ache* or *The Homecoming* is the total credibility of Disson as a personality, however incredible the things that happen to him may seem. Indeed, it is because Disson's rationale registers so fully that one senses the inadequacy of his responses to his situation— the failures don't fit precisely because Pinter has given us the man's measure so fully.

Unfortunately, the third woman in Disson's life, his wife Diana, is as oddly unsatisfying a figure as her brother. The dramatic point of the "conspiratorial postures" the guests at the tea-party appear to be adopting is that one is able to contrast these subjective impressions of Disson's with "objective" shots of the actual, innocent groupings over the cakes and buns. Yet Diana, like Willy, hovers uncomfortably between Disson's inner world of complex persecution, and the correlative world in which we see her behaving with undoubtedly suspicious-looking motives. The first distinctly uncomfortable moment in the play for Disson, in fact, is his objection to the twins' whispered giggling over breakfast, which is in turn related to something "Uncle Willy" has told them. [18] And Diana's reasons for wishing to be her brother's secretary remain obscure. [20]

It's possible, I suppose, that it is from these seeds of vague doubt that Disson's eventual, overwhelming feeling of being conspired-against blossoms. And there is certainly something grotesquely allusive about this brother-sister relationship, with all its memories of childhood summers and country gardens that Disson cannot share:

DISSON: Tell me about Sunderley.
WILLY: Sunderley?
DISSON: Tell me about the place where you two were born. Where you played at being brother and sister.
WILLY: We didn't have to play at being brother and sister. We were brother and sister.

DIANA: Stop drinking.

DISSON: Drinking? You call this drinking? This? I used to down eleven or nine pints a night! Eleven or nine pints! Every night of the stinking week! Me and the boys! The boys! And me! I'd break any man's hand for . . . for playing me false. That was before I became a skilled craftsman. That was before . . .

He falls silent, sits.

WILLY: Sunderley was beautiful.

DISSON: I know.

WILLY: And now it's gone, for ever.

DISSON: I never got there. [39–40]

Pinter is completely in control of his characters here. Disson's self-defence—note the self-reassuring repetitions of his inebriation, and even that accidental yet right-sounding inversion of the "eleven or nine pints"—thus harks back to the days "before I became a skilled craftsman", just as Willy and Diana are grieving for the lost days of a different youth. And, again, one senses the hidden depths of the play in the class antagonisms, the beer-swilling apprentice forever cut off from the beautiful children of the country-house. One had first recognised this in the contrast between Disson's stilted, conventional reply as bridegroom and Willy's polished suavity as best man. [14–16] And Disson's impulsive appointment of Willy to a job in his firm, as later his promotion to a partnership, [41] comes at a moment when, in his uncertainty of status, he feels the need to be able to patronise—not to be patronised—by a person he fears may be the "best man" indeed.

The problem is that too many of the play's subtleties are ill-fitted to the instantaneous, take-it-or-leave-it effect of the television medium. Even if one had the chance of returning again and again to a television play as one usually can (even if only in the study) to a good piece of writing for the stage, all the technical impedimenta of the piece present their own problems of assimilation. Each scene has its distinct physical location (in almost every room imaginable in Disson's house, in his own and in Willy's offices, in Disley's surgery), which is in a necessary, complementary relationship to the progress of Disson's malaise—creating the here-and-now from which he is becoming inexorably dissociated. And each has its televisual equivalent to a curtain-line, often deliberately anti-climactic, but a mark of dramatic punctuation none the less. Yet the constant shifts from one place to another, and the constant restructuring which follows each of these marks of punctuation, give *Tea Party* a kind of formal prolixity that is most unusual in Pinter's work—the more unusual in view of this play's closeness in date of composition to *The Homecoming*, which, whatever its faults, is seldom prolix. Here, the separate yet often closely identified other-world of Diana and Willy drifts like a fleeting glimpse of sunlight through the matted clouds of Disson's limited perception; and to this the bed-sitter-style secretary Wendy, the "oldest friend" Disley with his heavily, sexily bourgeois wife in tow, and the old-age-pinterers of Disson's parents, are very much more integral.

The pictures—the necessarily televisual pictures—are thus essential to the creation of points-of-view, yet they get in the way of the language as Pinter's *stage* pictures seldom do. (Teddy's ungainly omnipresence in the later scenes of *The Homecoming* is the blatant exception which proves this particular rule.) For usually Pinter's compression has amounted to the distilling of language and action into a quintessential version of reality: here, it seems to consist in the more straightforward compression of cramming as

many different things into the play as possible—mostly very
good things, in themselves—and hoping for the best. The
result is very far from Pinter's best. But *Tea Party* remains
intriguing in its allusiveness—fruitfully frustrating even, in
its refusal to be got to grips with. It is the only thing of its
kind in Pinter's dramatic canon to date, and the work,
perhaps, of a dramatist putting out feelers towards the
several possible directions his future creativity might take.

The sexual shape of *Tea Party* was a kind of eternal
quadrangle, whereas *The Basement*, first produced as a television play in February 1967, though conceived several
years earlier,[55] reconstitutes the more conventional triangle
of two men and a woman into a vicious circle. Law, sitting
at home in his basement flat in front of the fire, is knocked
up one rainy winter's night by his old but long unseen friend
Stott. Law invites his visitor to stay and Stott gratefully
accepts—going on to mention casually that he has left a
friend waiting outside. The friend turns out to be a girl,
Jane, with whom Stott forthwith climbs into Law's double-
bed. And in the course of the play, which seems to flash
backwards and forwards in time over some eighteen months,
Stott takes over the rest of the flat as well—whilst Law takes
over the girl. As the play ends, Stott, sitting at home in his
basement flat in front of the fire, is knocked up one rainy
winter's night by his old but long unseen friend Law. As
he invites him in, Stott cannot see Jane crouching in the
shadows. . . .

The play invites comparison with *Tea Party*, in its technical exploitation of the televisual medium, and, indeed,
adapts no better to stage performance. But it is the more
happily conceived work of the two in its total avoidance of
those matter-of-fact minutiae which occasionally obstructed
the movement of the earlier work. Here, surreal scenic

juxtapositions *illustrate* rather than obfuscate that stream of dramatic consciousness which was also to run through the three plays following it. Maybe it is even a sign of weakness that Pinter was over-dependent upon such illustrative techniques: but although the later plays were to need no such embellishment to their spoken words, here the illustrations are at least apposite, albeit not strikingly original. Thus, the exterior settings tend to be such as are beloved of the producers of television plays—airy cliff-tops and beaches, claustrophobic area-basements and backyards, frosty fields seen in long-shot. And indoors, that familiar, much fought-over room of Pinter's takes on a more anthropomorphic character than is usual in his later work, as its decorations switch back and forth, scene by scene, from Law's fairly old-fashioned comforts to the sixties-Scandinavian style of Stott's ascendancy, and, in the final scenes, from eastern exoticism to utter emptiness.

Drifting in time and space through all these settings are Law, Stott, and Jane, the two men variously indulging in schoolboyish trials of strength or athletic skill, or in less subtly sublimated struggles for the room and the girl. And, perhaps the crucial word in that last sentence is "schoolboyish". Jane, at least, makes a startling contrast to all or any of Pinter's earlier young women: she is "very young", [63] but the quality of her innocence—a sort of highly-sexed self-abnegation—is less her own than the product of some fifth-former's romantically erotic imagination. Thus, she seems to exist only as an object of the desires of Law and Stott—an object to seduce, to display oneself to, bodily or intellectually, or to send off to cook one's meals in between the self-indulgences of sex and showing-off. And yet this entirely fantasised girl is more real precisely because her existence is conceived as so precarious. If Ruth in *The*

Homecoming is the archetypal predatory female, Jane is an archetype of the adolescent sexual daydream. Neither is a "real" woman: but Jane's unreality is *realised* in dramatic terms, whereas Ruth's seems to have deceived Pinter as it is intended to deceive an audience.

The class-structure of the play is unusually hard to discern: the close friendship between Law and Stott is of the sort that suggests an Oxbridge or public-school origin, and their reminiscences seem to be of leisured undergraduate days— although the affluence which Law's vicariously boastful catalogue of Stott's possessions suggests he enjoys [64] doesn't square with the apparent penury of his arrival at the basement flat, or with the memories of that "awful place in Chatsworth Road", where the two men apparently once shared lodgings. [62] But Law's elaboration of Stott's supposed wealth and distinction is probably a device to alienate him from Jane: and in any case it would be a mistake to probe too closely into where Stott and Jane "really" come from. Out of nowhere, seemingly, into the here-and-now of the first scene in the basement—or, maybe, circuitously, out of the last scene of the play, the previous time around. For the action of *The Basement* is entirely self-contained, and, unlike *The Homecoming*, it never prompts one to query its premises.

Nevertheless, I think it's important to note that the first scene is not only the longest, but also the most hard-edged episode in the play. Thus, until Jane's first entrance, the dialogue is casual, nearly naturalistic: the two men talk about old times, Law gets Stott a towel to dry his hair, and Stott admits he's "looking for a place". [60] But then Jane appears, and the mood at once changes. Law wants to fetch her a towel, too. Stott offers her his used one, and wins the first tiny skirmish for sexual superiority when the girl takes it.

And from the moment of Law's calm acceptance of the couple getting into his bed together, the impartiality of realism gives way to impressionism. But *whose* impressions shape the scenes? Well, in brief, it is nearly always possible to relate the remainder of the play to the point-of-view of Law, but very seldom possible to see things through Stott's eyes, and never through those of the ethereal Jane.

The first episode in the flat, which has already lost its objectivity, finally dissolves as Law sits reading his *Persian Manual of Love*—impassive as the intruding couple begin to make love in his bed. Televisually, the experience is his, and there are very few subsequent scenes in which— dramatically as distinct from psychologically—he is not dominant. These later scenes begin by flashing forwards to the following summer and back again to winter—and there are three such seasonal sequences, each clearly specified. The earliest comprises the summer scene on the beach, as Law and Jane talk admiringly of Stott in his absence, [63–4] and a first flashback to winter—Stott and Jane still un- ashamedly amorous, and Stott beginning to extend his ambitions towards taking over the flat, getting Law to remove a picture he doesn't like as a first, symbolic step. The two men sit drinking lager and talking about Jane as the girl works in the kitchen. [65–6] Then follows a much quicker change. On the beach, Jane is caressing Law, but he is resisting her: and back in the wintry backyard, the girl announces lunch to the drinking couple. [66] Finally, in the last of this set of flashbacks, Jane and Law return together from the beach, towels over their shoulders, to find the room "unrecognisable". [67] Stott has made his takeover bid.

The following scene is a wintery one again: but it takes place in the "second furnishing", and I don't think it's being too pedantic to feel that this indicates a forward movement chronologically. For the relationships from this "time" onwards become less exploratory, the confrontations more open: and the contests between the two men begin to be directly competitive, increasingly violent—although it is always Stott who wins, by employing openly more vicious tactics each time. He first outploys Law in a pub conversation, [68] then makes him look ridiculous by failing at the last moment to join in a race they are running (for no apparent reason) across a field, with Jane as judge: Law, turning back to look for Stott, loses his balance, "stumbles, falls, hits his chin on the ground". [68–9] Back in the basement, now of oriental splendour, Stott and Law play a game of indoor cricket with marbles for balls and a flute for a bat, and the last marble of Stott's over strikes Law on the forehead and fells him. [73–5] Finally the two prepare to duel, in a room now entirely bare, with broken milk-bottles: but we witness only the preliminary sizing-up, and the scene ends as the bottles smash together in a sudden thrust. [77] After this, only the topsy-turvy return to the opening situation is to come: and the play closes as soon as it has shown in this way that its circle is closed.

The contests which suggest the "development" of the second part of the play are, however, interspersed with scenes in which the relationship between Law and Jane makes tentative progress, and there is, additionally, a highly ambiguous episode in which the couple attend Stott on what appears to be his deathbed. More significantly, there is one further flashback to the opening situation. This comes as a climax to three separate requests by Stott that Law should play a record on his hi-fi equipment: the first as he and Jane lie in bed smoking, during the winter of the "second furnishing", [67] the second presumably a little later, since Jane is now, like Law, in some sort of servitude

to Stott, [69] and the third during the summer, when Stott
finally specifies the record he wants—of Debussy. [70]
Pinter's stage direction reads:

> Law goes to the record cabinet. He examines record
> after record, feverishly, flings them one after the other at
> the wall. [70]

But when, finally, he picks out the right record, it is to turn
back to Stott and Jane as they climb naked into the bed in
the room as it was furnished first: and Law puts on the
record, dims the one lamp Stott hadn't turned out and "pokes
the dying fire".[56] This brief backwards-glance is surrounded
by summery scenes. Immediately afterwards, Law is watching Stott as he approaches Jane: then, as Jane "moves her
body away from him" Law calls out that he's "found the
record. The music you wanted." [71] But the Debussy
record is only finally seen revolving on its turntable between
the clashing of the broken milk bottles and the return to the
front area, as Law and Jane approach the flat where Stott
is sitting reading by the fire. [77]

The play is open to several interpretations or to none.
Those who prefer to assess the action as self-sufficient will,
in so doing, recognise the truth of its emotional development
—and thus also the assurance of the associated formal
tracery. And those who prefer to look for a reading between
the lines will, I think, find their response to the play enriched
by thus relating the action to situations within and beyond
its self-sufficiency—whether to comparable dramatic themes
of Pinter's, or to possible analogies in life.

The Basement may well prove to be Pinter's last work in
which a room-motif is of such considerable importance—
for here the feeling first expressed in *Night School* that the

girl invading the room may be better worth possessing than the place itself is crystallised. Law, actually or imaginatively, sacrifices the room for the girl, instead of giving up the girl, as Walter had in the earlier play, because of his obsession with the room.

But is Law's sacrifice actual or imaginary? As the play stands, it doesn't matter: it *happens*. But for what it's worth, my own impression of the action is as a make-believe in Law's mind, a fantasy he weaves in his chair by the fire. And this could almost as well have begun before Stott's arrival as afterwards, in some residual, hung-over jealousy or long-past puerility, except that the feeling of solidity about the play's first scene—that texturing of the here-and-now which is reconstructed only when the scene is itself reconstructed—makes for greater coherence if one conceives the "actual" arrival of Stott and Jane as the event which inspires Law to enact imaginatively his futuristic fantasy of sexual jealousy and possessiveness. Law, playing by the rules (it was Ronald Hayman[57] who pointed out the possibly literal implications of his surname), and with every appearance of reluctance, actually succeeds only in *letting* himself be seduced. This is itself against all the odds, which are weighted heavily by such suggestions of his sexual insufficiency as his lonely brooding over the *Persian Manual of Love*, his need, real or fantasised, to be titillated by the erotic come-hitherings of Jane, and his own reluctance to make any of the running. And that even this upside-down seduction is made to conform to a public-school code of honour—it is only Stott who cheats in the various contests, while Law himself plays the perfect host as well as the essentially perfect gentleman, even making as if to warn Stott against Jane's disloyalty to him [72]—reinforces one's impression of an adolescent quality about the sexual feelings manifested in the play, which is first sensed in the solipsistic nature of Jane herself.

Law's final speech in the opening scene reveals much about the quality of his living, and of his compensations for non-living:

> I was feeling quite lonely, actually. It is lonely sitting here, night after night. Mind you, I'm very happy here. Remember that place we shared? That awful place in Chatsworth Road? I've come a long way since then. I bought this flat cash down. It's mine. I don't suppose you've noticed the hi-fi stereo? There's all sorts of things I can show you. [62]

And Law unbuttons his cardigan, and "places it over the one lit lamp, so shading the light", [62] exactly as he does a second—surely the same—time midway through the play, when, after hurling record after record against the wall one summer's day, he turns with the single disc he's been searching for back into the winter's night of the opening scene. The speech here quoted is not, however, just important functionally (for its introduction of the hi-fi motif, and its veiled remembrances of things past), but for that typical avoidance of confronting others with one's own isolation— the admission of loneliness no doubt Law's hospitable attempt to make Stott and Jane feel they are not intruding, which has to be quickly covered up by the contradictory remark that he is really "very happy here".

One can't help contrasting the humanising quality of this instant-contradiction with the tricksy inversions of Max and Sam in *The Homecoming*—and noting how the "given" situation here is so much easier to accept for the emotional rightness of its formal shaping. One might add that such an interpretation as I have suggested—it's by no means the only interpretation which is consistent with this tantalisingly evocative script—is helpful not because it can be definitive, but because it serves as a possible objective correlative to a truly self-sufficient work of art: whereas the self-sufficiency of *The Homecoming* was isolative and isolating. But *The Basement* is, unfortunately, too well-made for its particular medium —the auto-destructive, galloping consumption of television being what it is—to survive as a major work of dramatic art.[58] It was, nevertheless, by adapting the technical devices he used here into an authorial manner of shaping a "legitimate" playscript that Pinter was able to weave the subjective reality of passing acquaintances, and their impact upon those they brush against, into the fabric of his dramatic dialogue in the plays which followed, and thus to achieve his best work since *The Caretaker*.

This is surely why *Landscape*, *Silence* and *Night* contrast at first sight so strangely with *Tea Party* and *The Basement*. Static actions on a simple set or bare stage, and a consequent dependence upon the human voice and manner alone, succeed the free-flowing movements of the television plays, with their employment of all the assistance of cinematic emphasis and of quick cutting between place and place or time and time that the medium of television could offer. The contrast is stranger because *Landscape* was first broadcast in April 1968, and—although it reached the stage in a double-bill with *Silence* at the Aldwych a year later—it might be persuasively argued that the medium of radio offered, potentially, even greater imaginative opportunities than Pinter had been taking on television. Yet I think it is helpful, in this case, to know that the play's only two characters, Beth and Duff, actually *are* sitting together in the same room, and not merely voices or memories alternating or occasion-

ally—almost—communicating in some limbo of lost memories. As so often in Pinter's work, *place* is vitally important
here—as it had even been in *The Dwarfs*, that least apparently
pinned-down of his plays, and the only one which does indeed
work better on radio than on the stage. Here the place is
"the kitchen of a country house". Against an indistinct
background of household impedimenta, Duff sits at the right
hand corner of the long kitchen table: and in an armchair,
at some distance to its left, sits his wife Beth. It is evening. [8]

A note prefacing the printed text of *Landscape* describes the
relationship between these two as follows:

Duff refers normally to Beth, but does not appear to hear
her voice. Beth never looks at Duff, and does not appear to
hear his voice. Both characters are relaxed, in no sense
rigid. [8]

The last instruction is, strictly speaking, superfluous, for
nothing that the couple say suggests tenseness or rigidity:
yet I suppose the unwary might just be tempted into solemn-
ising or ritualising the action—maybe conceiving it as a
sort of pastoral version of *The Basement*, in which a couple are
doomed to sit forever agonising over their circuitous reminiscences of love or of betrayal. But, in mood at least, Beckett's
Happy Days would make a more appropriate model—although
the happiness here is less overlaid with irony, the days less
regulated by the summoning bell. Besides, Duff's activities,
unlike Beckett's inert Willie's, are by no means confined to
the reading of small advertisements, while Beth's memories,
though just as wistful as Winnie's, seem more genuinely a
consolation in the here-and-now—for this couple aren't, of
course, stranded in an engulfing, nightmarish nowhere, but
in the kitchen of an otherwise deserted country house, for whose

absent owner they act as housekeepers-cum-caretakers. One more analogy, a formal one, and I promise to stop: perhaps *Landscape* is a comic lyric poem to Beckett's tragic epic? Such a relationship is *there*, but it is indeed as tenuous, even as tongue-in-cheek, as that between Homer and *Joseph Andrews*.

From the couple's "conversation" one gathers quite a lot about the landscape of *Landscape*—evidently a small country town, surely on or near the south coast, and, for my money, somewhere in Sussex. This precise identification of place is purely impressionistic—a matter of turns of phrase that ring true, of ruminative pauses, and of places with just the blending of the truly, genuinely rural and the artificial, uptight "county" that one senses in the slow certainties of Duff and in Beth's contempt for girls "squeaking in the hotel bar". [24] I imagine that each member of an audience will find his own location for *Landscape*: and its very title suggests that, if this was not Pinter's exact intention, he was certainly aware that his play was an evocation not merely of the things that have happened to his two characters, but of the place they have lived and loved in.

Structurally, *Landscape*'s one short act is made up of parallel monologues which, in defiance of the laws of dramatic geometry, occasionally make as if to touch one another. Beth's is most recognisably in the stream-of-consciousness manner, moving descriptively to and fro in time and space as *The Basement* had done visually. But here the time encompassed seems to be thirty-six hours or so at the most— and the space is no more than the distance between a crossroads where Beth's long-ago lover gave her a lift one morning in his car [21–2] and the beach to which the couple drove, and where they dawdled, swam, probably made love. There is, it's true, just an occasional backwards glance indoors, perhaps into this same house, where the acquaintance was first made, the first caress permitted. But whether the lover is that same Mr Sykes who, according to Duff, "took to us from the first interview", [20] or even the youthful Duff himself, is never revealed.[59] It scarcely matters. The affair was evidently a fleeting one, and it was over many years ago: but it has left a lingering, indelible trace in Beth's mind, the clear outlines of which she explores and, in so doing, restores. And the quality of the memory is both sensuous and sensual.

Duff meanwhile talks at his wife, needing her presence but no more than the illusion of her response. He speaks of his everyday activities: his walks around the park, his fishing, his visits to the pub, his arguments in the bar. He remembers, too, Beth as a young wife, the day he had confessed to her that he had been unfaithful and how she had forgiven him. Perhaps this was the time when Beth, in search of consolation, sought it in kind—at last letting her lover possess her body on the beach. Maybe this was the only time they made love. All the perhapses and maybes aren't important, however: the play is *there*, and the two characters, so alike and yet so different, are there, besides. The myths are there, too, for one's own making, from this rich yet resilient raw material.

Beth remembers her lover, and ignores her husband. Duff is happy in the trivial rounds of the present, and reshapes his wife's responses as he wishes. With his employer away, he can "walk down to the pub in peace and up to the pond in peace", [24] and although there is, of course, no answer when he asks Beth whether she likes him to tell her "about all the things that I've been doing", [21] he concludes that she does. He enjoys telling her, anyway.

But Beth herself needs no audience, not even an audience that isn't listening: maybe, for that matter, it is only her thoughts that she "speaks", not her words. Yet she is happy, too, worried only by the occasional awareness of growing old:

> Of course when I'm older I won't be the same as I am, I won't be what I am, my skirts, my long legs, I'll be older, I won't be the same. [24]

For all this, although she is already "a woman in her late forties", [8] Beth has changed little, and forgotten less, since she seduced her man, or was seduced by him, among the sand dunes. Duff, a few years older, has forgotten what he has chosen to forget—and he *has* chosen to forget the girl with whom he betrayed his wife. In confessing to her, he did not even admit who she was, or what she did:

> The girl herself I considered unimportant. I didn't think it necessary to go into details. I decided against it. [22]

Neither does he go into details now. He remembers only Beth's quiet forgiveness—which was maybe in truth a quiet desperation, driving her to give herself to her own lover. Maybe.

Maybe that lover has long since forgotten Beth too—considered *her* "unimportant"—and maybe the girl Duff loved and forgot remembers him and cherishes *his* memory, as Beth cherishes her own moment of wanting and being wanted. The play is open-ended, the possibilities unlimited. And within the framework of these possibilities the action is, as it were, one circumstance among many—which yet contains the many within itself. *Landscape* is at once an image, a perfect whole, and a tiny fragment. It is, indeed, a *landscape*, full of individual, pick-outable touches of truth—such as

Duff's entirely serious reflection concerning his walk in the park, that "the dog wouldn't have minded me feeding the birds" [11]—but true as a landscape painting is true, in a verisimilitude that is at once particular and representative.

There are two separate modes of being, two separate attitudes to experience, within the play. Dramatically, they are distinct yet interconnecting, both thematically—because Beth's remembered lover has probably forgotten her as Duff has chosen to forget his own brief inconstancy—and individually, because these two are part of one another's lives. The textures of their experience, richly rendered in Beth's sense of the intricacies of flesh and of all it touches, are thus made perceptible to Duff not in what he experiences, but in what he actively performs. The passive and active, the past and the present, are alike brought alive in their *words*—the woman, dramatically as sexually, complementary to the man.

Duff is a man of interests, whilst Beth, observing, is interested:

DUFF: So I thought I might as well pop in and have a pint. I wanted to tell you. I met some nut in there. First of all I had a word with the landlord. He knows me. Then this nut came in. He ordered a pint and he made a criticism of the beer. I had no patience with it.

BETH: But then I thought perhaps the hotel bar will be open. We'll sit in the bar. He'll buy me a drink. What will I order? But what will he order? What will he want? I shall hear him say it. I shall hear his voice. He will ask me what I would like first. Then he'll order the two drinks. I shall hear him do it. [15]

Here, Duff's encounter of the day before is about to catch him up in a detailed discourse on the intricacies of cellar-craft.

This has something of the same unexpectedly lyrical quality as Mick's do-it-yourself daydreaming in *The Caretaker*: but in this case the routines so lovingly described are the correct ones, the care which must be given to pulling a well-conditioned pint of beer both precisely and practically recreated. Beth, on the other hand, wasn't even sure, all those years ago, what drink to order: for her, simply observing her man, knowing that she will be asked what she wants to drink and that she will hear him ordering it, is wonder enough.

"People move so easily. Men. Men move." [9] This is the constant source of Beth's wonder, and her expression of it is her description of that movement:

When I watered the flowers he stood, watching me, and watched me arrange them. My gravity, he said. I was so grave, attending to the flowers. I'm going to water and arrange the flowers, I said. He followed me and watched, standing at a distance from me. When the arrangement was done I stayed still. I heard him moving. He didn't touch me. I listened. I looked at the flowers, blue and white, in the bowl.
Pause.
Then he touched me.
Pause.
He touched the back of my neck. His fingers, lightly, touching, lightly, touching, the back, of my neck. [13]

And this is only one of Beth's countless references to being touched. The use of the word as a euphemism for unsolicited sexual advances by Albert's alleged victim in *A Night Out*, and by Wendy in *Tea Party*, comes to mind: but here—as it does again in *Silence* and *Night*—physical touching suddenly becomes a tenderly recollected experience to middle-ageing women, not a cause of the shrinking-up of sexuality in young girls.

Maybe Beth's lover never did more than touch her. "He moved in the sand and put his arm around me. . . And cuddled me," is, at least, her most intimate admission. And these words are the climax to this particular, symphonic-style movement of her mind, which, after Duff's next inter-vention—or alternation—retraces its recollected emotions back to the beginning of the day, the catching of the bus to the crossroads, the walk in "the lane by the old church", the lift offered and accepted. [20–1]. It's as if, once the core of the experience has been relived, the surrounding circum-stances can be better, and more calmly, recalled and relished. Thus, as Beth's thoughts pick their way slowly forwards again, they light this time on tinier details of feeling and texture—on the bread that she had cooked herself, on the open windows of the car, [22] or on the technical intricacies of the drawing that served as an excuse for seeking out so desolate a spot on the beach:

I remembered always, in drawing, the basic principles of shadow and light. Objects intercepting the light cast shadows. Shadow is deprivation of light. The shape of the shadow is determined by that of the object. But not always. Not always directly. Sometimes it is only indirectly affected by it. Sometimes the cause of the shadow cannot be found. [27–8]

And this speech stands out, just a little obtrusively, as a statement of the play's own determining sensibility—its feel-ing for the shapes of the shadows thrown by the past, or sometimes by no discernible cause at all.

F

And so the play moves towards its conclusion, a penultimate note of the harshness from which Beth recoils struck by Duff's coarsely-phrased recollections of their reconciliatory lovemaking—in front of the dog, in the empty hall of the empty house:

> . . . you'll plead with me like a woman, I'll bang the gong on the floor, if the sound is too flat, lacks resonance, I'll hang it back on its hook, bang you against it swinging, gonging, waking the place up, calling them all for dinner, lunch is up, bring out the bacon, bang your lovely head, mind the dog doesn't swallow the thimble, slam—[29]

Then, in climactic counterpoint, comes Beth's lyrical evocation of that gentler lovemaking, or maybe merely of the tender touching of a man and a woman on a beach:

> He lay above me and looked down at me. He supported my shoulder.
> *Pause.*
> So tender his touch on my neck. So softly his kiss on my cheek.
> *Pause.*
> My hand on his rib.
> *Pause.*
> So sweetly the sand over me. Tiny the sand on my skin.
> *Pause.*
> So silent the sky in my eyes. Gently the sound of the tide.
> *Pause.*
> Oh my true love I said. [29–30]

Here, Duff's abrupt, hurtful monosyllables contrast forcefully with the languorous, rising and falling caresses of Beth's "tender . . . softly . . . sweetly . . . tiny . . . silent . . . gently". "Objects intercepting the light cast shadows", and in *Landscape* it is surely the past, intercepting the present, that casts its shadow over the action. The "shape of the shadow" may perhaps be determined by the actual, remembered forms of the past: or it may be that "the cause of the shadow cannot be found", except in deep-felt longings and unrealised desires. But at the point of intersection between present and past—or between activity and passivity, harshness and gentleness, substance and shadow, male and female: there lies the reality and the waking dream of *Landscape*.

Night—a ten-minute two-hander which was included in a programme of eight similarly short pieces called *Mixed Doubles* at the Comedy Theatre in April 1969—is a kind of coda to *Landscape*. But in mood, as well as in its extreme brevity, it is closer to the style of the early revue sketches than any of Pinter's intervening work: and thematically it is concerned with a less complex form of non-communication than Beth and Duff's. "A man and a woman in their forties" are remembering over their bedtime cups of coffee the first time they met. [54] It was at a party: afterwards, the Man offered to escort the Woman home, and on the way they made love.

WOMAN: And you had me and you told me you had fallen in love with me, and you said you would take care of me always, and you told me my voice and my eyes, my thighs, my breasts, were incomparable, and that you would adore me always.
MAN: Yes I did.
WOMAN: And do you adore me always.
MAN: Yes I do.
WOMAN: And then we had children and we sat and talked

and you remembered women on bridges and towpaths
and rubbish dumps.

MAN: And you remembered your bottom against railings
and men holding your hands and men looking into your
eyes.

WOMAN: And talking to me softly.

MAN: And your soft voice. Talking to them softly at night.

WOMAN: And they said I will adore you always.

MAN: Saying I will adore you always. [60–1]

Thus the play ends—with a summing-up of the disagreement that is at the core of its bare, brittle action. Did the
couple pause and pet on a bridge, as the Man remembers,
or embrace against the park railings, as the Woman claims?
Did the Man really take her breasts in his hands? Or was
it "another night perhaps. Another girl?" [59]

And how much does it matter or interest us anyway?
Granted that this is an occasional piece, more anecdotal and
even (in the manipulation of the anecdote) more formulaic
than the revue sketches, one senses that here Pinter was
merely toying with those varieties-of-the-same-experience so
much more deftly elaborated in *Landscape* and *Silence*. Yet,
were the manner a little less heavily modulated and the
idiom a little less casually controlled, this might almost be a
study of Beth and Duff at some ten-years-earlier stage of
mutual dissociation.

Here, the streams of consciousness have not yet diverged,
and so differing versions of the truth clash against one another
as they do in *Old Times*, whereas in *Landscape* they brush
as gently as shadows intercepting. The Woman, too, has
Beth's feeling for translating tender actions into gentle words,
whilst the Man, like Duff, is harsher, more abrupt, in sen-
suality and vocabulary alike:

WOMAN: You took my face in your hands, standing by the railings. You were very gentle, you were very caring. You cared. Your eyes searched my face. I wondered who you were. I wondered what you thought. I wondered what you would do.

MAN: You agree we met at a party. You agree with that? [56–7]

And again:

MAN: A man called Doughty gave the party. You knew him. I had met him. I knew his wife. I met you there. You were standing by the window. I smiled at you, and to my surprise you smiled back. You liked me. I was amazed. You found me attractive. Later you told me. You liked my eyes.

WOMAN: You liked mine.

Pause.

You touched my hand. You asked me who I was, and what I was, and whether I was aware that you were touching my hand, that your fingers were touching mine, that your fingers were moving up and down between mine.

MAN: No. We stopped on a bridge. I stood behind you. I put my hand under your coat, on to your waist. You felt my hand on you. [57–8].

But such features, such distinctions, only begin to be meaningful in the retrospective context of *Landscape*. There are one or two hints of the broader horizons of that earlier play— the wife at the party, perhaps, who "looked at you dearly, as if to say you were her dear" [58]—but the irony underpinning the whole action, of a pair who vowed to adore each other always but can't even agree where the vow was made, cannot sustain more than a superficial interest. By itself, *Night* is more truly a sketch than the revue sketches: for they were self-contained, whereas here the only interest beyond the anecdotal—and the play *is* interesting on that rather self-limiting level—lies in the evidence it reveals of current concerns Pinter explored satisfyingly, instead of tantalisingly, in *Landscape* and *Silence*.

And the rest, almost, is *Silence*. First performed in a double-bill with *Landscape* at the Aldwych in July 1969, this, too, is a play about touching—about human beings consoled or repelled by contact, reinterpreting moments of meeting according to their own sensibilities, and giving verbal shape to the shadows cast by their own pasts and presents. Here there are three characters—two men, Rumsey and Bates, and the woman who walks or once walked out with both of them, Ellen. The sexual situation is a familiar, triangular one. Ellen wants, or once wanted, the evidently older man—for Rumsey once took her walking when she was a little girl, [41] and now cherishes that memory more than the reality of the love the grown woman offers, or once offered, to him. "Find a young man," he tells her. "There aren't any," Ellen replies. [44] There is only Bates—who is put up with (even, it seems, occasionally slept with) for want of a better. But Bates, wanting no better, senses that he is himself insufficient, and sinks back into the loneliness of a "childish old man, suffocating himself" with the memories, or the re-enactment, of his failures. [43]

Each character is living his or her whole life instantaneously, so that whether any particular experience belongs to childhood, youth or middle-age is often difficult to determine. Indeed, it is best regarded as . . . just an experience. But the elderly personae, necessarily more particularised,

are most readily picked out—Ellen, perhaps, living alone
in her room, and occasionally quizzed by her "drinking
companion" about

> the sexual part of my youth. I'm old, I tell her, my
> youth was somewhere else, anyway I don't remember. [36]

And in a sense this is true. Ellen doesn't remember: she
re-lives. But Bates feels all the burden of his own middling
years, and confuses past and present only because their
rhythms of boredom and frustration are the same—whilst
Rumsey, already a man when Ellen was a girl, wears his old
age lightly. Utterly self-centred, his selfishness is yet concealed from himself as it is from others: for he is a man who
has grown used to being needed, and he supplies the needs
others have for him because this enables him to sense and to
give shape to his own existence. Now he, like Ellen and Bates,
is alone, remembering, re-experiencing.

For his set, Pinter simply specifies "three areas. A chair
in each." [32] And only on a few occasions does a character
move out of his or her isolation into an enacted memory of
a meeting with another, in a recollected past that becomes
the stage present. Rumsey, ruminative and contented, looks
after his house, tends his animals: he enjoys Ellen's company,
relishing her malleability to his moods, her dressing for his
eyes. Bates is less contentedly adjusted, uncomfortable in his
noisy lodgings yet compulsively drawn to the noise of the
nearby town—where, perhaps, Ellen can be more easily
and accessibly seduced. "How many times standing clenched
in the pissing dark waiting?" [35] And Ellen is enigmatic,
sometimes an enigma to herself—introspective and with-
drawn, yet as puzzled about her own feelings as she can be
perceptive about them:

> After my work each day I walk back through people but I don't notice them. I'm not in a dream or anything of that sort. On the contrary. I'm quite wide awake to the world around me. But not to the people. There must be something in them to notice, to pay attention to, something of interest in them. In fact I know there is. I'm certain of it. But I pass through them noticing nothing. It is only later, in my room, that I remember. Yes, I remember. But I'm never sure whether what I remember is of today or of yesterday or of a long time ago. [46]

In such a chronologically uncertain manner, Ellen and Rumsey do most of the talking—self-analytically etching-in their emotions, whereas Bates, wearily resigned or aggressively impulsive, blurts out phrases as curt and unreflecting as his actions. Bates speaks once to Ellen, and Ellen twice to Rumsey: but these brief crossings of the borders apart, the characters talk only to themselves, ignoring yet isolated by the passage of time.

The essence of each is caught in the opening speeches they are given. In Rumsey's

> I walk with my girl who wears a grey blouse when she walks and grey shoes and walks with me readily wearing her clothes considered for me. [33]

Surely among the most simply evocative opening lines ever spoken in a play. In Ellen's immediate consciousness of being sought by two men, of her own preference for one of them:

> There are two. One who is with me sometimes, and another. He listens to me. I tell him what I know. We

walk by the dogs. Sometimes the wind is so high he does
not hear me. I lead him to a tree, clasp closely to him and
whisper to him, wind going, dogs stop, and he hears me.
[33–4]

And in Bates's brusque memoranda:

Caught a bus to the town. Crowds. Lights round the market,
rain and stinking. Showed her the bumping lights. Took
her down around the dumps. Black roads and girders.
She clutching me. This way the way I bring you. Pubs
throw the doors smack into the night. Cars barking and
the lights. She with me, clutching. [34]

Instantly, these three characters, their environment, their
relationships, are caught: and, prismatically, the play reflects one against another, distorts one individual's being
by catching it within the consciousness of another. The set
designed by John Bury for the original production, an
elaborate confusion of mirrors at once multiplying angles
of vision and entrapping the reflected images in a maze of
memory, could scarcely have been more exact or appropriate.

The three characters of *Silence* are, then, as closely inter-
related as they are distinguished one from another. All have
the countryman's awareness of the weather, and climatic
images cluster. Rumsey observes the weather, fits it into his
scheme of things:

It is curiously hot. Sitting weather, I call it. The weather
sits, does not move. I shall walk down to my horse and
see how my horse is. He'll come towards me. [39]

Whereas Bates—"standing clenched in the pissing dark waiting"—merely endures the weather as another misfortune. Rumsey is proud of the need animals, like human beings, seem to have for him—yet the speech just cited closes with a rare, quickly stifled moment of doubt on this subject:

> Perhaps he doesn't need me. My visit, my care, will be like any other visit, any other care. I can't believe it. [39]

And soon this is amplified into the most self-aware speech Rumsey is allowed in the play:

> Sometimes I see people. They walk towards me, no, not so, walk in my direction, but never reaching me, turning left, or disappearing, and then reappearing, to disappear into the wood. [40]

This is precisely the nature of Rumsey's human contacts, the semantic shift between "towards me" and "in my direction" quintessential to his personality, which repels closeness as it invites and requires reliance.

But if these moments of truth only once or twice ruffle Rumsey's bland assurance, for Bates the moments when the tension ebbs are the exceptions:

> Funny. Sometimes I press my hand on my forehead, calmingly, feel all the dust drain out, let it go, feel the grit slip away. Funny moment. That calm moment. [41]

The play ends, as it began, with a contrast between Rumsey, walking in the country, and Bates, catching his bus to the town—and, throughout, this has set the tone for a careful counterpointing of mood and of dialogue. Consider this less "significant" but representative snatch of dialogue:

> RUMSEY: Pleasant alone and watch the folding light. My animals are quiet. My heart never bangs. I read in the evenings. There is no-one to tell me what is expected or not expected of me. There is nothing required of me.
> BATES: I'm at my last gasp with this unendurable racket. I kicked open the door and stood before them. Someone called me Grandad and told me to button it. It's they should button it. Were I young . . . [35]

But it's always been the same. For Rumsey, the peace, the sense of others needing him, placating his pride without disrupting his easy, selfish routine. For Bates, the unendurable racket, whether it is the escape from loneliness or the sharp reminder of it: the failure to find solace in the noise of the town, or silence in the countryside.

And *Silence* remains rooted, like *Landscape*, in the countryside. Even the silence of its title is not that of some apocalypse of the absurd, or even that of an extended pinteresque pause, but, surely and simply, the silence of the countryside at night—its quality of peace, which Bates so desperately seeks. As in *Landscape*, the openings for individual extrapolation are almost unlimited, but the significance of the title is one point on which the play does declare itself. The preciseness and the ambiguity combine in this pivotal speech of Ellen's:

> Around me sits the night. Such a silence. I can hear myself. Cup my ear. My heart beats in my ear. Such a silence. Is it me? Am I silent or speaking? How can I know? Can I know such things? No one has ever told me.

I need to be told things. I seem to be old. Am I old now?
No one will tell me. I must find a person to tell me these
things. [43]

These, then, are night thoughts, thoughts which are the
more resonant for the silence engulfing them—and more in
need of reassurance and of certainty. Bates is denied any
such comfort. Ellen has sought and thinks she has found it
in the one who "listens to me". But for that one, for Rumsey,
the silence is as sufficient as the self.

Silence is set, in my own private mythology, to the west of
Landscape, in Dorset, maybe, or in Wiltshire—its accents less
overladen with genteel vowels, yet its neighbourhood still
near enough to urban cacophony for its own peacefulness to
be a matter for comment rather than merely a fact of life.
Any such place will do, so long as it's more truly rural than
the slightly self-conscious small town of *Landscape*, but at the
same time accessible and with a sense of its own values—
which are more dignified, and, above all, *different* from those
of the town in which Bates has tried and failed to lose himself. "They ask me where I come from. I say of course from
the country," says Ellen. [47] Of course from the country—
from the farm where Rumsey and Bates work, or once
worked:

There are two. They halt to laugh and bellow in the
yard. They dig and punch and cackle where they stand.
They turn to move, look round at me to grin. I turn my
eyes from one, and from the other to him. [45]

And "the other" is, of course, poor, put-upon Bates—kept
awake by the noise and driven to frustrated fury by the sexual
energy of his fellow-lodgers, pitied by his landlady, barely

tolerated by Ellen. "Sleep? Tender love? It's of no importance," is his small, self-deceiving consolation. [51]

Thematically, *Silence* is less complex than *Landscape* because its three characters are working over the same ground and have experienced the same events and patterning of relationships within the play's "simultaneous" time structure. Its actual complexity lies in the personalised, private interpretations each has of these events, and in the light each interpretation throws upon the others—and, again, in the sense of place that is evoked on a totally bare or at most suggestively set stage. From the minutely detailed yet clearly symbolic settings of his early plays, Pinter has thus come exactly half-circle, employing here a setting which is abstract, or could equally well be non-existent—yet giving his action a physical, though verbally-realised, location that is, in itself, free from associations other than those the characters draw from or impose upon it. The allegorical actions of *The Room* or *The Birthday Party* have at last evolved into the totally self-defining actions of *Landscape* and *Silence*.

The trouble with Pinter's most recent play, *Old Times*, first produced at the Aldwych in June 1971, is that it *lacks* the self-defining quality of *Landscape* and *Silence*. It is set precisely, almost pedantically—indeed, it is in part a play *about* pedantry—in a fashionably converted farmhouse, somewhere near the sea. For no apparent reason, the bedroom of the second act is a symmetrical mirror-image of the sitting-room in which the first is set, and where a dinner is to be shared by Deeley and his wife Kate with Anna, a friend of Kate's last seen some twenty years ago. Inevitably and properly, much of the evening is taken up with reminiscences about old times. But here tricks of memory are too evidently those played by the dramatist rather than those experienced by his characters, and the moments encapsulated in one individual's recollections, only to be warped into another's mould of memory later in the play, suggest the complications less of the human mind than of verbal scribean devices, carefully planted for later plucking. The peculiarly specific qualities of *Landscape* and *Silence* derive from what is said, not from where the action is physically set: here, the explicit visual trappings necessitate the verbal trickery, and one is reminded, uncomfortably, of the emotional trickery of a play like *The Homecoming* besides.

Anna thus has to stand immobile by the up centre window while Kate and Deeley go through an introductory, expository scene anticipating her arrival—wondering how she's altered, whether she's married, or a vegetarian, or undergone other traumatic changes in twenty years. She cuts into this conversation quite effectively, as if at coffee following the meal, but her earlier presence would be question-begging were it not clearly just a convenient technical device for maintaining the continuity of the action. Throughout, what seemed a satisfactory merging of time-scales in *Landscape* and *Silence* here becomes merely a means of avoiding anything so old-fashioned as flashbacks. And where an overlap does seem to be intended, it is more reminiscent of Priestley than of Pirandello in everything but solemnity of pretension.

Crucially, there seems no good reason why the memories of these characters should be any more at variance now than twenty years ago: one knows, for that matter, insufficient about either state to be quite sure which is which, or what has changed. Did Deeley really desire Anna as well as Kate? Did Anna desire Kate in her own deceptively prim fashion, while not exactly repelling Deeley's voyeuristic advances? Did Kate, tenuous as her very existence sometimes seems to become, ever manage to focus her emotions sufficiently to desire anybody? The play ends as Deeley, slumped in an armchair and exhausted by his own quiet sobbing, seems to acknowledge his exclusion from the self-sufficiency of the women: but whether the scene is taking place in visual affirmation of what Kate claims happened twenty years ago, or is a ritual re-enactment of it in the present—or is maybe even an acknowledgement of what never happened but appropriately might have—remains ambiguous. The last words of the play have already been spoken by Kate, about the man who slept in Anna's bed after a death that "had all happened elsewhere":

He asked me once, at about that time, who had slept in that bed before him. I told him no one. No one at all. [73]

So not only the nature of Anna's death, "alone and dirty"—and cleanliness is important to Kate, whose nightly bath separates the play's two short acts—but also her very existence is finally called in question. Like the other questions, it is unanswered, unanswerable.

Curiously, this hazily-directed action concerns very clear-cut people. Indeed, part of the trouble with the play may be that its characters have to impose their own sophistication over what might otherwise be a true stream-of-consciousness: and Pinter is evidently aware that this poses problems. Thus, he has Deeley—down-to-earth yet out to impress—forever lingering over the meaning of words, their appropriateness or rarity:

ANNA: Ah, those songs. We used to play them, all of them, all the time, late at night, lying on the floor, lovely old things. Sometimes I'd look at her face, but she was quite unaware of my gaze.

DEELEY: Gaze?
ANNA: What?
DEELEY: The word gaze. Don't hear it very often. [26]

But where Deeley is glibly forthcoming yet vulnerable, his wife is outwardly quiescent yet inwardly self-contained. She rather relishes being talked about, affectionately, as if she weren't there—occasionally surfacing to make a feeble protest, but quietly proud of the dream-like quality that Deeley and Anna clearly, mistakenly relish in her. In one of her few speeches of more than a sentence or two, Kate contextualises this:

> The water's very soft here. Much softer than London. I always find the water very hard in London. That's one reason I like living in the country. Everything's softer. The water, the light, the shapes, the sounds. There aren't such edges here. And living close to the sea too. You can't say where it begins or ends. That appeals to me. I don't care for harsh lines. [59]

Yet if the absence of "edges" and "harsh lines" makes the world of *Old Times* seem many miles indeed from the edgy, harsh London of *The Homecoming*, in fact the play depends on much the same kind of distortion of normal motives and responses.

There is even a "key speech" such as Ruth's in *The Homecoming*—assigned, appropriately, to Anna the outsider in this very different domestic situation:

> There are some things one remembers even though they may never have happened. There are things I remember which may never have happened but as I recall them so they take place. [32]

Now it's true that Anna, also, is precisely characterised, and that the hopeful stab at metaphysics here is typical of her calculated yet elliptic manner—an effect of effortless superiority which is actually quite an effort to maintain. Unfortunately, this remark also seems philosophically pivotal to what the play "means"—indeed, it is solemnly reproduced at the beginning of the jacket blurb of the printed text, as if to reassure us that *this* is what it's all about. No such reassurance was needed in *Landscape* and *Silence*, and, significantly, none was attempted—as if Pinter felt confident that these plays needed no formulaic gloss to keep their audiences alert and involved. Motifs of memory, too, here recur either tricksily or for blatantly comic effect, or both—so that *Odd Man Out*, the Robert Newton film at which Deeley may or may not have first met Kate, crops up clumsily again when Anna, contrary to Deeley's version of the story, claims, very much as a conversational ploy, to have been there too. [38]

The comedy is, thankfully, usually more effective than the trickery:

DEELEY: So it was Robert Newton who brought us together, and it is only Robert Newton who can tear us apart.
    Pause.
ANNA: F. J. McCormick was good too.
DEELEY: I know F. J. McCormick was good too. But he didn't bring us together. [30]

A lot of the less *significant* conversation is also quietly funny, and there are touches of pure Pinter:

ANNA: You have a wonderful casserole.
DEELEY: What?

ANNA: I mean wife. So sorry. A wonderful wife.

DEELEY: Ah.

ANNA: I was referring to the casserole. I was referring to your wife's cooking.

DEELEY: You're not a vegetarian, then?

ANNA: No. Oh no.

DEELEY: Yes, you need good food in the country, substantial food, to keep you going, all the air . . . you know.

Pause. [20–21]

The thought-processes here are exactly rendered into the lazy formalities of casual conversation. Note the slightly over-insistent correction of a slip of the tongue—Deeley's helpful changing of the subject itself insufficiently thought out, so that it lapses into that splendidly unmeaningful final remark. But such observation is too often blurred by the need to generate plot—and to work towards that final vignette of Deeley in his armchair, the women lying on their divans, maybe in a country farmhouse in the present, maybe in a London bed-sit twenty years ago. Human memory, sacrosanct in its very imperfections in *Landscape* and *Silence*, is here no more than the dramatist's plaything: and such over-reliance upon the tricks of his trade yet again permits what has once been fruitfully ambiguous in Pinter's work to degenerate into the merely mechanical and arbitrary. Thankfully, his powers of recovery from such lapses into self-parody are also proven: and his occasional bad play thus has at least the virtue of bringing his next good play one step nearer the stage.

CONCLUSION

Conclusion

ONE OF the problems with Pinter's plays is that of a consummately skilful craftsman who has very little sense of his own art. Hence, on the one hand, the assurance with which Pinter notates his scripts with those idiosyncratic silences, pauses and elliptic dots—and, on the other, his nearly total inability to rise above superficialities in assessing what his plays might mean or, more to the point, *matter*. In this, he is, of course, very much an actor's playwright—as Nigel Dennis has observed:

All Pinter plays are like elaborations of the drama school exercise, when the student is told (say), "You are alone in a room. Suddenly, the door opens. You see a man standing there. O.K. Now you improvise the rest."

The test for the student is to conduct the make-believe that follows with sincerity and conviction. Any text that he or she may improvise is negligible—any *words* will do provided they will supply a motive for moving, or sitting transfixed, for pausing or blustering, for registering emotion, for building an atmosphere . . . All playwrights must think themselves into their characters in order to put life into them. Mr Pinter is perhaps the first playwright to think himself exclusively into the actor: it is this that he is "obsessed with".

Dennis goes on to argue that a typical Pinter exchange is

> virtually meaningless in thought or intellect, but put two
> good actors on the stage and see how it will hum—what
> deep significance, what frightening overtones, what enig-
> matic images it will produce. It is perfectly legitimate
> theatre, of a childish sort, and it is God's gift to the acting
> profession. An actor is not concerned with what something
> is about: he is only interested in how he can act. In
> Mr Pinter he has found a playwright who is equally
> uninterested in what the work is about: the work is simply
> the acting thereof.

This is a disenchanted view, but there is some truth in it:
at least, it serves a healthily corrective purpose. For at his
most pinteresque, Pinter *does* fall into a formula guaranteeing
an instant response—a mannered ringing of empty exchanges
fraught with seeming significance. Yet at his best the plays
are resonant with the proliferating possibilities and mysteries
of life—and, less expectedly, with a feeling for humanity,
whether in extremity or at its most humdrum, that rewards
with new insights at each fresh acquaintance.

I have stressed throughout this book that relatively little
is to be gained from a Pinter play at a first sitting. One can
be merely baffled at a relatively simple but promising piece
of work, as were critics taken unawares by the first production
of *The Birthday Party*: or one can be deceived by the apparent
profundity of a work such as *The Homecoming* which, on
closer examination, proves to be hollow in the middle. Once
one *knows the story*, either its interest is exhausted, or its
tensions, no longer concerned with "what happens next",
become those of ever more intricately known human relationships. This is why I find the assumptions behind such a

defence of *The Homecoming* as this of John Russell Taylor's
so implausible:

> The play is entirely self-defining: an immaculate demon-
> stration of Pinter's own expressed ideal, the play which
> has nothing to do with the becauses of drama, but unrolls
> imperturbably in terms of the simple "and then . . . and
> then . . . and then" of a children's tale. In it he seems to
> have attained a new certainty, a new directness in his
> expression which appears to tell us all and yet in the end
> tells us nothing except the play itself, the unparaphrase-
> able, irreducible artistic whole.[60]

This is criticism based on a coinage which Nigel Dennis
effectively turned on its flip side, revealing a curious view
alike of drama and of children's tales (one might as persuasively argue that children's literature is a succession of
"why . . . because" constructions, responding to the search
for explanations that is incessant in the child, and thwarted
in the adult whenever art expresses willing ignorance before
the seeming purposelessness of existence). But the analogy is,
in any case, based on the false premise that it is the story-
telling element in Pinter that matters most—that adds up to
the "irreducible artistic whole". And this I would dispute:
the story matters, as in myth, because of the ways in which
it allows the characters to relate to us through circumstances
which, in themselves, are already familiar—the familiarity
either that of everyday life, or of an earlier acquaintance
with the play itself.

On the whole, Pinter's characters are not hovering at the
edge of reality over some abyss of existential horror: rather,
they are arguing over the minutiae of everyday existence
or troubled by the missed opportunities or the sheer

irrecoverability of the past, trying to take such measure of their lives as will make them manageable. There is a human necessity to define boundaries—not necessarily through any territorial imperative dimly sensed by naked apes, but as part of the innately human quest for self-awareness, which, at its simplest, is a process of self-definition. The more vulnerable the human being, the more fearful he will be lest that definition, once accomplished in however primitive a form, should be subjected to personal or social pressures for hurtful change. It is the fear of such change that makes Pinter's earliest plays redolent not with menace—which implies external forces actively lurking—but with the disruption that threatens where the boundaries of individual propriety are *already* crossed, as in farce, and the necessity for adjustment comes into conflict with the pressing instinct for inertia in spite of everything.

But self-containment, defined dramatically, is a virtue only if it is formally appropriate, as it was to Pinter's early plays—the tragi-farces, their actions truly the most "irreducible artistic wholes" Pinter has achieved. In his second burst of creative activity, he was more concerned with characters whose would-be self-contained lives were already being stretched under pressure of circumstances—yet who were ill-equipped to cope with the need for social reciprocity thus imposed upon them. Consider Albert in *A Night Out*, Aston and Davies in *The Caretaker*, or Walter in *Night School*: and note how in those plays a tentative *patterning* of relationships emerges—not with false geometric precision, but with a feeling for the many-sidedness of personality, alike in its accommodations to circumstance and in the adjustments made by the *other* parties in the many confrontations.

It doesn't particularly matter who comes off best: for life, ultimately, still has to be got on with. Hence, although the struggle for dominance may, as Pinter has conceded, be a "repeated theme in my plays",[61] at its most expressive it is not an abstract, chessboard struggle, or a staking of territorial claims in an emotional jungle, but an exploration of the consequences of interaction between people engaged in usually insignificant endeavours that may not seem particularly civilised but are always, for better or worse, the *products* of civilisation—as also, demonstrably, are Albert, Davies and Walter.

Sadly, there followed a period during which such a sense of connection between Pinter's plays and humankind's experience slackened: as at an earlier stage of his career, in *A Slight Ache*, a genuine reflection of manners tended to distort itself into a mere collection of mannerisms. And when Pinter emerged from what was, in *The Homecoming*, a trough in more senses than one, it was to return to the search for self-containment—now enacted amidst the petit-bourgeoisie, in fashionably furnished apartments or well-appointed country houses. It's important to emphasise both the recognisable quality of Pinter's most recent characters, and the sense of society that has evolved surely from the earlier, hemmed-in worlds of the living-wombs. For if Pinter's plays are mythic, archetypal, or whatever, the myths and the archetypes are those of *our* time, not tarnished versions of heroic originals in some vanished golden age: and so it is the truths they tell about our time, rather than any possible handing down of eternal truths, that matters. The earliest plays thus *allegorise* contemporary life, whilst the middle plays *formalise* it, occasionally to excess—and the most recent explore it in terms of the mental images men make of themselves to encapsulate and so make bearable their lives. It is not so much Pinter's audiences who share a "desire for verification" as his characters—whether for the doubtful reassurance of Davies's old insurance cards, or the truth of remembered love in *Landscape* and *Silence*.

I commented when discussing *Landscape* that Beth creates an exact miniature of the incident she is recollecting before elaborating its details. And this is not only dramatically appropriate, as the way memory is likely to work, but also theatrically helpful—for it gives an audience, too, the whole picture, before filling in the finer shades of what is, precisely, a verbal landscape. It is, perhaps, as if Pinter himself were here aware of the need to *know the play whole*—and, in *Old Times*, the opening exposition serves much the same purpose, albeit here blurring rather than highlighting the detail of the subsequent action. Similarly, he sometimes seems to recognise the "desire for verification" by slotting-in an explicatory speech which actually underlines itself as the philosophical gist of the play—Ruth's speech about movement in *The Homecoming*, Anna's speech about memory in *Old Times*. Sometimes, as in these two cases, this is a mark of a play's weakness to establish its own implicit credentials—whereas in the cases of Aston's monologue in *The Caretaker* and of the conflicting ideologies of *The Dwarfs*, the philosophical gloss fits naturally into the way the action is developing. Certainly, it is in those plays where mystification seems to have become an end in itself—besides *The Homecoming*, in *The Collection* and *Old Times*, Pinter's most pirandellian works—that the desire becomes, for an audience, most insistent—whereas, in *The Birthday Party* or *Silence*, the element of elusiveness is integral and contained, adding to the possibilities of fruitful interpretation rather than reducing them to a search for the "right" solution.

I have not devoted much attention in the present study to stylistic aspects of Pinter's language, nor to such allegedly unifying themes as that of the whore-mother, apotheosised in Ruth. Martin Esslin has discussed the former with great distinction, and failed utterly to convince me of the existence (let alone the importance) of the latter.[62] I have ignored Pinter's five published screenplays,[63] because they present problems of formal approach that require a work I would not feel qualified to write—whereas it is, I think, significant that Pinter's plays for radio and television are formally very much closer to his original work for the theatre. Indeed, almost every broadcast play has eventually been adapted for stage performance—and it's notable that, *Tea Party* and *The Basement* excepted, Pinter has chosen to publish the texts of these adaptations rather than the radio or television scripts.

This takes us back to that concern for notation of the printed word and for scrupulousness of stage direction that is one of the few ways in which Pinter comes closer to John Arden that to most of his other contemporaries. Pinter's self-estimate is pertinent:

> I think, you see, that this is an age of such overblown publicity and overemphatic pinning down. I'm a very good example of a writer who can write, but I'm not as good as all that. I'm just a writer. . . .[64]

So he is: a very good example of a writer who can write. I am, in the last analysis, not quite so confident that Pinter's work will survive to "classic" status as Osborne's or Arden's—and he himself declares that "it's of no moment to me". For, so like yet so unlike his fellow Jewish writer Arnold Wesker, he is very much a man of his times, and writes for them—and for the actors who act in them. In another half a century there is the danger that performers may have lost the capacity to play Pinter as irrecoverably as we have today grown out of sympathy with the style of an Irving or a Tree, or even of a Wolfit.

Pinter is, then, an actor's playwright, with all the virtues and limitations that implies. He will, of course, continue to write—and, I suspect, continue to move disconcertingly from the master work of each period of his stylistic development to a formulaic *reductio ad absurdum* of the same manner. But he will remain, I think, a lyrical writer, choosing to ignore the possibilities of the narrative element in drama, continuing to write strong curtains—and continuing, above all, to write a play around a hard kernel of situation, enwrapping this in arbitrary layers of ambiguity at his worst, but at his best showing us the kaleidoscopic multiplicity of attitude, ambivalence, distortion and doubt that is the individual's attempt to bring reality within the bounds of personality, and so to make it bearable.

APPENDICES

APPENDICES

Notes and References

Works of which fuller details are given in the Bibliography are here cited by their short titles only.

1 See Harold Pinter, "Speech: Hamburg 1970", *Theatre Quarterly*, I, iii, 1971, 3–4.
2 I am indebted for this catalogue of pomposities about Pinter to Nigel Dennis, "Pintermania", *New York Review of Books*, 17th December 1970, 21–2.
3 See the interview with Harold Pinter in *Theatre at Work*, ed. Charles Marowitz and Simon Trussler, 108.
4 In his chapter on "Compressionism" in *Drama in the Sixties* (London: Faber, 1966, 45–74), Laurence Kitchin helpfully suggests the tradition from which this aspect of Pinter's work derives—not least helpfully indicating that it *is* a tradition, not the dramatist's own innovation.
5 Terence Rattigan's attempt to "interpret" *The Caretaker* led to probably the best known of Pinter's resolute refusals to admit exegesis. "Feeling rather pleased with myself," Rattigan recalls, "I said, 'It's the Old Testament God and the New Testament God, with the Caretaker as humanity—that's what it's all about, isn't it?' Pinter said, 'It's about two brothers and a caretaker.'"
6 This assumption underlies most of Pinter's comments on his work. But see, in particular, "Speech: Hamburg 1970", *op. cit.*, *passim*, and the interview in *Theatre at Work*, 104–5.

7 See Martin Esslin, *The Peopled Wound*, London: Methuen, 1970, 11–31.

8 See, for example, Ronald Hayman, *Harold Pinter*, 7, or John Russell Taylor, *Anger and After*, 326–8.

9 Cf. my remarks on this kind of play in the Introduction to my *Plays of John Whiting* (London: Gollancz, 1972), 14.

10 See the interview in *Theatre at Work*, 97–8.

11 In *The Theatre of the Absurd* (London: Eyre and Spottiswoode, 1962). Martin Esslin describes Pinter as "one of the most promising exponents of the Theatre of the Absurd in the English-speaking world".

12 See "The Comedies of Menace" in Alrene Sykes, *Harold Pinter*, 1–36.

13 Pinter himself has remarked that the arrival of "an intruder to upset the balance of everything" should not be considered "an unnatural happening. . . . This thing, of people arriving at the door has been happening in Europe in the last twenty years. Not only the last twenty years, the last two to three hundred." Quoted in Martin Esslin, *The Peopled Wound*, 36.

14 See John Russell Taylor, *Anger and After*, 326.

15 Thus, an interpretation which diminishes Stanley's centrality, and gives more weight to the roles of his fellow lodgers, helps to meet Ronald Hayman's objection to the third act as "something of a letdown" in *Harold Pinter*, 25.

16 See, for example, Bernard F. Dukore, "The Theatre of Harold Pinter", 48

17 See my *Plays of John Whiting, op. cit.*, 27.

18 See the interview in *Theatre at Work*, 106.

19 *Ibid.*, 98.

20 *Ibid.*, 104.

21 Cf. my *Plays of John Whiting, op. cit.*, 47–8.

22 See for example, John Russell Taylor, *Anger and After*, 329–30. And Ronald Hayman, in *Harold Pinter*, 17, claims of *both* the gunmen, "we don't feel they really want to know any more than they do".

23 Martin Esslin, in *The Peopled Wound*, 69–85, aptly reminds us of Pinter's conscientious objection to National Service, with its equal insistence upon the unquestioning carrying-out of orders from possibly unknown superiors. Yet Esslin's reading of the action as taking place in a dream-world where the "supernatural forces driving us to murder our fellow human being" come to the surface seems to me to ignore the crucial element of free-will in the play—towards which Gus is struggling and which Ben is *voluntarily* subjugating.

24 "Edward's fate is closely analogous to Rose's in *The Room*," claims Martin Esslin in *The Peopled Wound*, 90. "She too is visited by a symbolic figure who had been waiting for her outside. She too is stricken with blindness and presumably loses her warm home to be expelled into the cold of the basement: death." But if the Matchseller is demonstrably a "symbolic figure", the blind Negro is also and always a *blind Negro*. Besides, being stricken with blindness is different from being struck dead—though whether *significantly* different, in the dramatic context of *A Slight Ache*, is admittedly arguable.

25 This oft-cited remark of Pinter's originally appeared in a programme note to *The Room* and *The Dumb Waiter*, which is reprinted in full in *The Peopled Wound*, 40.

26 Martin Esslin, in *The Peopled Wound*, 82, points out that Pinter used an episode from his abandoned play *The Hothouse* as the basis for this sketch. Cf. Pinter's own remarks on *The Hothouse* in the interview in *Theatre at Work*, 104.

G

27 Others are reprinted in an American acting edition, *The Dwarfs and Eight Revue Sketches*, and in the other sources cited in the Bibliography, below.

28 Thus, of *The Black and White*, Pinter has explained that he had "never done anything with the tramp women because they fitted naturally into a complete play which just happened to be four minutes long". Quoted in John Russell Taylor, *Anger and After*, 333–4.

29 See the interview in *Theatre at Work*, 98.

30 Pinter himself modified the play's climax. It was his original intention that the action should culminate "with the violent death of the tramp".

31 Quoted in Martin Esslin, *The Theatre of the Absurd*, 217, from a radio interview given by Pinter to Kenneth Tynan in 1960.

32 See the interview in *Theatre at Work*, 105–6.

33 *Ibid.*, 105.

34 Cf. Martin Esslin, in *The Peopled Wound*, 105.

35 See, for example, Ronald Hayman, *Harold Pinter*, 36.

36 See John Russell Taylor, *Anger and After*, 343–4.

37 *Ibid.*

38 Earlier, Pinter had co-directed *The Collection* with Peter Hall, but the double-bill of *The Dwarfs* and *The Lover* was the first London production for which he was solely responsible.

39 Martin Esslin's chapter on *The Dwarfs*, in *The Peopled Wound*, 117–25, provides some interesting comparisons between the novel and the dramatic version—which are not, however, strictly relevant to its success as a play in its own right.

40 See the interview in *Theatre at Work*, 101.

41 *Ibid.*

42 Cf. Lenny's preoccupation with the nature of "a table"

in *The Homecoming*. "All right, I say, take it, *take* a table, but once you've taken it, what you going to do with it?"

43 Martin Esslin offers a diametrically opposite interpretation in *The Peopled Wound*, 119. "It is the desolation of the young man emerging from the wild whirlpool of steaming adolescence into the bare, ordered world of respectability." This, although Len is *in his thirties*.

44 See Martin Esslin, *The Theatre of the Absurd*, 220.

45 See Ronald Hayman, *Harold Pinter*, 47.

46 Martin Esslin, in *The Peopled Wound*, 129, claims that "*any* of the different versions of the incident around which *The Collection* revolves may be true—or none. The point is that we have an abundance of possible motivations for each possible version." It is surely in this very abundance that any "point" becomes blunted.

47 See John Russell Taylor, *Anger and After*, 353.

48 See the interview in *Theatre at Work*, 103.

49 Conflicting interpretations abound. A good sampling of viewpoints can be found in John Lahr's *Casebook on Harold Pinter's "The Homecoming"*, but the most important critical analysis is Martin Esslin's, in *The Peopled Wound*, 137–57. My disagreements with Mr Esslin here are so profound and far-reaching that it would be profligate of space to attempt a detailed rebuttal of his case, which seems to me to argue for the "archetypal" basis of *The Homecoming* at the same time as explaining it away as a work of realism by special pleading that makes the action about as untypical as it could conceivably be. I can only leave the reader to make his own comparisons.

50 Nigel Dennis aptly describes Pinter's handling of pavlovian dramatic devices in his review article "Pintermania", cited under Note 2, above.

51 Cf. Ronald Hayman, *Harold Pinter*, 66.

52 John Russell Taylor, in *Anger and After*, 355, agrees at least that "there is no moral framework by which what happens can be judged", though he regards the play as "a work of dazzling directness and simplicity". Esslin argues for its "immense relevance"—Hayman, on the other hand, that it is "gratuitously unpleasant".

53 See the interview in *Theatre at Work*, 100.

54 Pinter's refusal to admit a narrative element into *Tea Party* is the more significant since the play actually originated as a short story. Martin Esslin, in *The Peopled Wound*, 157–62, compares the two versions.

55 *The Basement* was intended for production as one of a sequence of three projected films, the others to be by Beckett and Ionesco. Only Beckett's *Film* was actually made. See Martin Esslin, *The Peopled Wound*, 162.

56 Martin Esslin, in *The Peopled Wound*, 162–8, compares *The Basement* with its source material—the prose fragment *The Examination* and the prose-poem *Kullus*—in both of which the room is "symbolised by the fire in the grate".

57 See Ronald Hayman, *Harold Pinter*, 73.

58 This was written before I saw the stage version of *The Basement*, in a double-bill with *Tea Party*: but I think that that production bore out my assessment of the limited stage potential of the play.

59 *Since* writing the play, Pinter has decided that Duff was the man on the beach, and that Beth and Sykes were never lovers. See *The Peopled Wound*, 192.

60 See John Russell Taylor, *Anger and After*, 356.

61 See the interview in *Theatre at Work*, 105.

62 See Martin Esslin, "Language and Silence", in *The Peopled Wound*, 193–224.

63 For details see the Bibliography, below, "Screen plays".

64 See the interview in *Theatre at Work*, 108.

Harold Pinter

1930　10th October. Born in Hackney, East London. His father was Hyman Pinter, a tailor, and his mother Frances, born Mann. Early childhood spent in this working-class area, "in a brick house on Thistle-thwaite Road, near Clapton Pond".

1939　Evacuated during the early part of the war to "a castle in Cornwall . . . with twenty-four other boys", and later, with his mother, "to a place closer to London".

1944　Returned to London, and attended Hackney Downs Grammar School. Played Macbeth and Romeo in school productions.

1947　Left school.

1948　Attended R.A.D.A., erratically and briefly. Two tribunals turned down his application to be registered as a conscientious objector.

1949　Called up for National Service, and twice appeared before a magistrate for refusing to enter the army. Fined on both occasions. "The magistrate was slightly sympathetic." Began to write *Kullus*, a "prose poem in dialogue".

1950　First poems published in *Poetry London*. Small acting parts in radio features. Began work on the unpublished novel, *The Dwarfs*.

1951　Attended Central School of Speech and Drama, and

from September worked with Anew McMaster's Shakespeare touring company in Ireland for a year.

1953 Appeared in Donald Wolfit's classical season at the King's Theatre, Hammersmith.

1954 Assumed the stage name David Baron, and began several years in repertory in the south of England, finding odd jobs as waiter, doorman, dish-washer and salesman between engagements.

1956 Married the actress Vivien Merchant while playing opposite her in Bournemouth.

1957 His first play, *The Room*, written at the instigation of the actor Henry Woolf for performance by the Drama Department of Bristol University, while Pinter was working in repertory in Torquay. Began work on *The Birthday Party* immediately afterwards.

1958 *The Birthday Party*, well-received on tour by Oxford and Cambridge audiences, flopped at the Lyric Theatre, Hammersmith, closing after one week. Moved to Chiswick, London. His son Daniel born.

1959 *The Dumb Waiter* premiered in Germany. *A Slight Ache* broadcast. *A Night Out* completed, for broadcasting in the following March. Wrote the revue sketches for *One to Another*.

1960 *The Room* and *The Dumb Waiter* staged in a double-bill at Hampstead Theatre Club in January, and transferred to the Royal Court in March. Television productions of *The Birthday Party* and *A Night Out*. *The Caretaker* staged at the Arts Theatre Club, and transferred for a long West End run to the Duchess Theatre, winning *Evening Standard* award. *Night School* televised in July. *The Birthday Party*, first of his plays to be seen in the United States, produced at the Actors' Workshop, San Francisco. The radio play *The Dwarfs* broadcast.

1961 Stage versions of *A Slight Ache* and *A Night Out*. Television production of *The Collection*. Pinter took over role of Mick for four weeks in *The Caretaker* before its New York production, which received the Page One Award of the Newspaper Guild of New York.

1962 Stage version of *The Collection*, under his own and Peter Hall's direction, began Pinter's association with the Royal Shakespeare Company. Screenplay for *The Servant*, from Robin Maugham's novel, directed by Joseph Losey.

1963 *The Lover* televised. Film version of *The Caretaker*, directed by Clive Donner. Directed *The Lover*, in a double-bill with *The Dwarfs*, at the Arts Theatre Club. *The Lover* received the Prix Italia for Television Drama at Naples, and awards from the Guild of British Television Producers and Directors.

1964 Screenplay of *The Servant* received British Screenwriters Guild Award. Screenplay for *The Pumpkin Eater*, from Penelope Mortimer's novel, directed by Jack Clayton, which received British Film Academy Award in 1965. Directed revival of *The Birthday Party* at the Aldwych Theatre.

1965 *Tea Party* televised. London production of *The Homecoming* at the Aldwych. Paris production of *The Collection* and *The Lover*, as a double-bill. Pinter played role of Garcia in Sartre's *Huis Clos* on BBC Television.

1966 Awarded C.B.E. in Birthday Honours List. Paris production of *The Homecoming*. Screenplay for *The Quiller Memorandum*, from Adam Hall's novel *The Berlin Memorandum*, directed by Michael Anderson.

1967 New York production of *The Homecoming*. Television production of *The Basement*, as a film script in 1963. Screenplay for *Accident*, from Nicholas Mosley's novel, directed by Joseph Losey. Directed *The Man in the Glass Booth*, by Robert Shaw, at the St Martin's Theatre. *The Homecoming* received Tony Award for Best Play on Broadway, and New York Drama Critics Award. Moved to house near Regents Park.

1968 *Landscape* broadcast in April. Film version of *The Birthday Party*, directed by William Friedkin. New York stage productions of *Tea Party* and *The Basement*. Published *Mac*, a memoir of Anew McMaster.

1969 Screenplay for *The Go-Between*, from L. P. Hartley's novel, directed by Joseph Losey. *Night* staged in the anthology-programme, *Mixed Doubles*, at the Comedy Theatre, and *Landscape* and *Silence* in a double-bill at the Aldwych.

1970 Directed James Joyce's *Exiles* at the Mermaid Theatre. *Tea Party* and *The Basement* staged in a double-bill at the Duchess Theatre.

1971 Screenplay for *The Go-Between* received major award at Cannes Film Festival. *Old Times* staged at the Aldwych. Directed Simon Gray's *Butley* at the Criterion Theatre.

1972 Revival of *The Caretaker*, directed by Christopher Morahan, at the Mermaid Theatre.

Cast Lists

The Birthday Party

Directed by Peter Wood. Designed by Hutchinson Scott. First London performance at the Lyric Theatre, Hammersmith, on 19th May 1958.

Petey	..	..	..	..	Willoughby Gray
Meg	..	..	..	..	Beatrix Lehmann
Stanley	..	..	..	..	Richard Pearson
Lulu	..	..	..	..	Wendy Hutchinson
Goldberg	..	..	..	..	John Slater
McCann	..	..	..	..	John Stratton

Directed by Harold Pinter. Designed by Ralph Koltai. First London performance of this revival by the Royal Shakespeare Company at the Aldwych Theatre on 18th June 1964.

Petey	..	..	..	..	Newton Blick
Meg	..	..	..	..	Doris Hare
Stanley	..	..	..	..	Bryan Pringle
Lulu	..	..	..	..	Janet Suzman
Goldberg	..	..	..	..	Brewster Mason
McCann	..	..	..	..	Patrick Magee

A Slight Ache

Directed by Donald McWhinnie. First broadcast performance on the BBC Third Programme on 29th July 1959.

| Edward | .. | .. | .. | .. | Maurice Denham |
| Flora | .. | .. | .. | .. | Vivien Merchant |

Directed by Donald McWhinnie. Designed by Brian Currah. First stage performance as part of a triple-bill entitled *Three* at the Arts Theatre on 18th January 1961.

Edward	..	..	..	..	Emlyn Williams
Flora	..	..	..	..	Alison Leggatt
The Matchseller	..	..	..		Richard Briers

The Room

Directed by Anthony Page. First London performance in a double-bill with *The Dumb Waiter* at the Hampstead Theatre Club on 21st January 1960. This production transferred to the Royal Court Theatre on 2nd March 1960.

Bert Hudd	..	..	..	Howard Lang
Rose	..	..	..	..	Vivien Merchant
Mr Kidd	..	..	..	..	Henry Woolf
Mr Sands	..	..	..	..	John Rees
Mrs Sands	..	..	..	..	Auriol Smith
Riley	..	..	..	..	Thomas Baptiste

In the production at the Royal Court Theatre, the part of Bert Hudd was played by Michael Brennan, that of Mr Kidd by John Cater, that of Mr Sands by Michael Caine, and that of Mrs Sands by Anne Bishop.

The Dumb Waiter

Directed by James Roose-Evans. First London performance in a double-bill with *The Room* at the Hampstead Theatre Club on 21st January 1960. This production transferred to the Royal Court Theatre on 2nd March 1960.

Ben	Nicholas Selby
Gus	George Tovey

A Night Out

Directed by Donald McWhinnie. First broadcast performance on the BBC Third Programme on 1st March 1960.

Albert Stokes	Barry Foster
Mrs Stokes	Mary O'Farrell
Seeley	Harold Pinter
Kedge	John Rye
Barman at the Coffee Stall ..	Walter Hall
Old Man	Norman Wynne
Mr King	David Bird
Mr Ryan	Norman Wynne
Gidney	Nicholas Selby
Joyce	Jane Jordan Rogers
Eileen	Auriol Smith
Betty	Margaret Hotine
Horne	Hugh Dickson
Barrow	David Spenser
The Girl	Vivien Merchant

Directed by Philip Saville. First television performance networked by ABC Television on 24th April 1960.

Albert Stokes	Tom Bell
Mrs Stokes	Madge Ryan
Seeley	Harold Pinter
Kedge	Philip Locke
Barman at the Coffee Stall ..	Edmond Bennett
Old Man	Gordon Phillott
Mr King	Arthur Lowe
Mr Ryan	Edward Malin
Gidney	Stanley Meadows
Joyce	José Read
Eileen	Maria Lennard
Betty	Mary Duddy
Horne	Stanley Segal
Barrow	Walter Hall
The Girl	Vivien Merchant

Directed by Leila Blake. Designed by Brian Currah. First stage performance as part of a triple-bill entitled *Counterpoint* at the Comedy Theatre on 2nd October 1961.

Albert Stokes	Brian Peck
Mrs Stokes	Anna Wing
Seeley	Rodney Bewes
Kedge	Walter Hall
Barman at the Coffee Stall ..	Douglas Harris
Old Man	Peter Hutton
Mr King	Trevor Reid
Mr Ryan	William Stephens
Gidney	Glyn Houston
Joyce	Patricia Marks

Eileen	..	..	..	..	Patricia Denys
Betty	..	..	..	..	Gabrielle Beaumont
Horne	..	..	..	..	Nicholas Pennell
Barrow	..	..	..	..	Michael Slater
The Girl	..	..	..	..	Jeanne Mockford

The Caretaker

Directed by Donald McWhinnie. Designed by Brian Currah. First London performance at the Arts Theatre on 27th April 1960. This production transferred to the Duchess Theatre on 30th May 1960.

Mick	..	..	..	..	Alan Bates
Aston	..	..	..	..	Peter Woodthorpe
Davies	..	..	..	..	Donald Pleasence

Directed by Christopher Morahan. Designed by Eileen Diss. First London performance of this revival at the Mermaid Theatre on 2nd March 1972.

Mick	..	..	..	..	John Hurt
Aston	..	..	..	..	Jeremy Kemp
Davies	..	..	..	..	Leonard Rossiter

Night School

Directed by Joan Kemp-Welch. First television performance networked by Associated Rediffusion on 21st July 1960.

Annie	..	..	..	..	Iris Vandeleur
Walter	..	..	..	..	Milo O'Shea
Milly	..	..	..	..	Jane Eccles

Sally	..	..	..	..	Vivien Merchant
Solto	..	..	..	..	Martin Miller
Tully	..	..	..	..	Bernard Spear

Directed by Guy Vaesen. First broadcast performance on the BBC Third Programme on 25th September 1966.

Annie	..	..	..	..	Mary O'Farrell
Walter	..	..	..	..	John Hollis
Milly	..	..	..	..	Sylvia Coleridge
Sally	..	..	..	..	Prunella Scales
Solto	..	..	..	..	Sydney Tafler
Tully	..	..	..	..	Preston Lockwood
Barbara	..	..	..	..	Barbara Mitchell
Mavis	..	..	..	..	Carol Marsh

The Dwarfs

Directed by Barbara Bray. First broadcast performance on the BBC Third Programme on 2nd December 1960.

Len	..	..	..	..	Richard Pasco
Pete	..	..	..	..	Jon Rollason
Mark	..	..	..	..	Alex Scott

Directed by Harold Pinter. Designed by Brian Currah. First stage performance in a double-bill with *The Lover* at the Arts Theatre on 18th September 1963.

Len	..	..	..	..	John Hurt
Pete	..	..	..	..	Philip Bond
Mark	..	..	..	..	Michael Forrest

The Collection

Directed by Joan Kemp-Welch. First television performance networked by Associated Rediffusion on 11th May 1961.

Harry	..	..	..	..	Griffith Jones
James	..	..	..	..	Anthony Bate
Stella	..	..	..	..	Vivien Merchant
Bill	..	..	..	..	John Ronane

Directed by Peter Hall and Harold Pinter. Designed by Paul Anstee and John Bury. First stage performance in a double-bill with Strindberg's *Playing With Fire* by the Royal Shakespeare Company at the Aldwych Theatre on 18th June 1962.

Harry	..	..	..	..	Michael Hordern
James	..	..	..	..	Kenneth Haigh
Stella	..	..	..	..	Barbara Murray
Bill	..	..	..	..	John Ronane

The Lover

Directed by Joan Kemp-Welch. First television performance networked by Associated Rediffusion on 28th March 1963.

Richard	..	..	..	..	Alan Badel
Sarah	..	..	..	..	Vivien Merchant
John	..	..	..	..	Michael Forrest

Directed by Harold Pinter. Designed by Brian Currah. First stage performance in a double-bill with *The Dwarfs* at the Arts Theatre on 18th September 1963.

Richard	..	..	..	..	Scott Forbes
Sarah	..	..	..	..	Vivien Merchant
John	..	..	..	..	Michael Forrest

Tea Party

Directed by Charles Jarrott. First television performance on BBC Television on 25th March 1965.

Disson	..	..	..	..	Leo McKern
Wendy	..	..	..	..	Vivien Merchant
Diana	..	..	..	..	Jennifer Wright
Willy	..	..	..	..	Charles Gray
Disley	..	..	..	..	John le Mesurier
Lois	..	..	..	..	Margaret Denyer
Father	..	..	..	..	Frederick Piper
Mother	..	..	..	..	Hilda Barry
Tom	..	..	..	..	Peter Bartlett
John	..	..	..	..	Robert Bartlett

Directed by James Hammerstein. Designed by Una Collins. First London stage performance in a double-bill with *The Basement* at the Duchess Theatre on 17th September 1970.

Disson	..	..	..	..	Donald Pleasence
Wendy	..	..	..	..	Vivien Merchant
Diana	..	..	..	..	Gabrielle Drake
Willy	..	..	..	..	Barry Foster
Disley	..	..	..	..	Derek Aylward
Lois	..	..	..	..	Jill Johnson
Father	..	..	..	..	Arthur Hewlett
Mother	..	..	..	..	Hilda Barry
Tom	..	..	..	..	Robin Angell
John	..	..	..	..	Kevin Chippendale

The Homecoming

Directed by Peter Hall. Designed by John Bury. First stage performance by the Royal Shakespeare Company at the Aldwych Theatre on 3rd June 1965.

Max	..	..	..	Paul Rogers
Lenny	..	..	..	Ian Holm
Sam	..	..	..	John Normington
Joey	..	..	..	Terence Rigby
Teddy	..	..	..	Michael Bryant
Ruth	..	..	..	Vivien Merchant

The Basement

Directed by Charles Jarrott. First television performance on BBC Television on 20th February 1967.

Stott	..	..	..	Harold Pinter
Jane	..	..	..	Kika Markham
Law	..	..	..	Derek Godfrey

Directed by James Hammerstein. Designed by Una Collins. First London stage performance in a double-bill with *Tea Party* at the Duchess Theatre on 17th September 1970.

Stott	..	..	..	Barry Foster
Jane	..	..	..	Stephanie Beacham
Law	..	..	..	Donald Pleasence

Landscape

Directed by Guy Vaesen. First broadcast performance on the BBC Third Programme on 25th April 1968.

| Beth | .. | .. | .. | .. | Peggy Ashcroft |
| Duff | .. | .. | .. | .. | Eric Porter |

Directed by Peter Hall. Designed by John Bury. First stage performance in a double-bill with *Silence* by the Royal Shakespeare Company at the Aldwych Theatre on 2nd July 1969.

| Beth | .. | .. | .. | .. | Peggy Ashcroft |
| Duff | .. | .. | .. | .. | David Waller |

Night

Directed by Alexander Doré. Designed by Tim Goodchild. First stage performance as part of an entertainment entitled *Mixed Doubles* at the Comedy Theatre on 9th April 1969.

| Man | .. | .. | .. | .. | Nigel Stock |
| Woman | .. | .. | .. | .. | Vivien Merchant |

Silence

Directed by Peter Hall. Designed by John Bury. First stage performance in a double-bill with *Landscape* by the Royal Shakespeare Company at the Aldwych Theatre on 2nd July 1969.

Ellen	..	..	..	..	Frances Cuka
Rumsey	..	..	..	..	Norman Rodway
Bates	..	..	..	..	Anthony Bate

Old Times

Directed by Peter Hall. Designed by John Bury. First stage performance by the Royal Shakespeare Company at the Aldwych Theatre on 1st July 1971.

Deeley	..	..	..	..	Colin Blakely
Kate	..	..	..	..	Dorothy Tutin
Anna	..	..	..	..	Vivien Merchant

Bibliography

WORKS BY HAROLD PINTER

PLAYS

The Room. In *The Birthday Party and Other Plays*, London: Methuen, 1960; and in *The Birthday Party and The Room*, New York: Grove Press, 1961.

The Birthday Party. London: Encore Publishing Company, 1959. In *The Birthday Party and Other Plays*, London: Methuen, 1960; and in *The Birthday Party and The Room*, New York: Grove Press, 1961.

The Dumb Waiter. In *The Birthday Party and Other Plays*, London: Methuen, 1960; in *The Caretaker and The Dumb Waiter*, New York: Grove Press, 1961; and in *New English Dramatists 3*, ed. Tom Maschler, Harmondsworth: Penguin Books, 1961.

A Slight Ache. In *A Slight Ache and Other Plays*, London: Methuen, 1961; and in *Three Plays*, New York: Grove Press, 1962.

A Night Out. In *A Slight Ache and Other Plays*, London: Methuen, 1961; and in *A Night Out, Night School, Revue Sketches*, New York: Grove Press, 1968.

The Revue Sketches. "Trouble in the Works", "The Black and White", "Request Stop", "Last to Go", and "Applicant" in *A Slight Ache and Other Plays*, London: Methuen, 1961; and in *A Night Out, Night School, Revue Sketches* New York: Grove Press, 1968. These, and additionally "Interview" and "That's All, That's Your Trouble", in *The Dwarfs and Eight Revue Sketches*, New York: Dramatists

Plays Service. "Dialogue for Three" in *Stand*, VI, iii, 1963. "Special Offer" in Arnold P. Hinchliffe, *Harold Pinter*, New York: Twayne 1967.

The Caretaker. London: Methuen, 1960. In *The Caretaker and The Dumb Waiter*, New York: Grove Press, 1961.

Night School. In *Tea Party and Other Plays*, London: Methuen, 1967; and in *A Night Out, Night School, Revue Sketches*, New York: Grove Press, 1968.

The Dwarfs. In *A Slight Ache and Other Plays*, London: Methuen, 1961; and in *Three Plays*, New York: Grove Press, 1962.

The Collection. In *The Collection and the Lover*, London: Methuen, 1963; and in *Three Plays*, New York: Grove Press, 1962.

The Lover. In *The Collection and The Lover*, London: Methuen, 1963; and in *The Lover, Tea Party, The Basement*, New York: Grove Press, 1967.

The Homecoming. London: Methuen, 1965. New York: Grove Press, 1966.

Tea Party. In *Tea Party and Other Plays*, London: Methuen, 1967; and in *The Lover, Tea Party, The Basement*, New York: Grove Press, 1967.

The Basement. In *Tea Party and Other Plays*, London: Methuen, 1967; and in *The Lover, Tea Party, The Basement*, New York: Grove Press, 1967.

Landscape. In *Landscape and Silence*, London, Methuen: 1969, and New York: Grove Press, 1970.

Night. In *Landscape and Silence*, London: Methuen, 1969, and New York: Grove Press, 1970; and in *Mixed Doubles*, London: Methuen, 1970.

Silence. In *Landscape and Silence*, London: Methuen, 1969, and New York: Grove Press, 1970.

Old Times. London: Methuen, 1971. Grove Press, 1971.

SCREENPLAYS

Five Screenplays. London: Methuen, 1971. Contains the screenplays for *The Servant*, based on the novel by Robin Maugham; *The Pumpkin Eater*, based on the novel by Penelope Mortimer; *The Quiller Memorandum*, based on the novel *The Berlin Memorandum* by Adam Hall; *Accident*, based on the novel by Nicholas Mosley; and *The Go-Between*, based on the novel by L. P. Hartley.

SHORT STORIES AND VERSE

Rural Idyll and *European Revels.* In *Poetry London*, No. 20, November 1950. Poems.

One a Story, Two a Death. In *Poetry London*, No. 22, Summer 1951. Poem.

The Examination. In *The Collection and The Lover*, London: Methuen, 1963. Short story.

Tea Party. In *Playboy*, January 1965. Short story.

Poems, selected by Alan Clodd. London: Enitharmon Press, 1968. Omits the early poems cited above, but includes the prose poem *Kullus.*

Memories of Cricket. In *Daily Telegraph Magazine*, 16th May 1969.

PERSONAL AND CRITICAL WRITINGS

"Writing for Myself", in *Twentieth Century*, CLXIX, 1961, 172–5.

"Pinter Between the Lines", in *The Sunday Times*, 4th March 1962, 25. Reprinted as "Writing for the Theatre" in *Evergreen Review*, No. 33, 1964, 80–2.

"*The Birthday Party*" in *Writers' Theatre*, ed. Willis Hall and Keith Waterhouse, London: Heinemann, 1967, 69.

Mac. London: Enitharmon Press, 1968. Memoir of Anew McMaster.

"Speech: Hamburg 1970", in *Theatre Quarterly*, I, iii, 1971, 3–4.

INTERVIEWS

In *New Theatre Magazine*, II, 1961, 8–10. An interview with Harry Thompson, entitled "Harold Pinter Replies".

In *Transatlantic Review*, No. 13, Summer 1963, 17–26. An interview with Kenneth Cavander, entitled "Filming *The Caretaker*", reprinted in *Behind the Scenes*, comp. Joseph F. McCrindle, New York: Holt, and London: Pitman, 1971.

In the *Daily Mail*, 7th March 1964. An interview with Marshall Pugh, entitled "Trying to Pin down Pinter".

In *The Paris Review*, X, No. 39, 1966, 13–37. An interview with Lawrence M. Bensky, reprinted in *Theatre at Work*, ed. Charles Marowitz and Simon Trussler, London: Methuen, 1967, and New York: Hill and Wang, 1968, 96–109.

In *Sight and Sound*, Autumn 1966. An interview with John Russell Taylor.

In *The New Yorker*, XLIII, 25th February 1967, 34–6. An interview in "Talk of the Town", entitled "Two People in a Room".

In *The Saturday Review*, 8th April 1967, 57. An interview with Henry Hewes, entitled "Probing Pinter's Play".

In *The Evening Standard*, 25th and 26th April 1968. An interview with Kathleen Tynan, entitled "In Search of Harold Pinter".

In *First Stage*, VI, Summer 1968, 82. An interview with William Packard.

In *The Listener*, 6th March 1969. An interview with Michael Dean, first broadcast on BBC Television.

WORKS ABOUT HAROLD PINTER

Bibliographies

Lois G. Gordon, "Pigeonholing Pinter: a Bibliography", in *Theatre Documentation*, I, i, 1968, 3–20.

Helen H. Palmer and Anne Jane Dyson, "Harold Pinter", in *European Drama Criticism*, Hamden, Connecticut: Shoe String Press, 1968, 314–17.

Herman T. Schroll, *Harold Pinter: a Study of his Reputation (1958–1969) and a Checklist*, Metuchen: Scarecrow Press, 1971.

These are particularly useful for tracking down reviews of original London and New York productions of Pinter's plays, in periodicals and in "quality" newspapers. In addition, Miss Gordon's bibliography provides brief synopses of many of the more general articles cited below. Martin Esslin's *The Peopled Wound* contains a select list of translations of Pinter's plays into other languages.

Symposia

John Lahr, ed., *A Casebook on Harold Pinter's "The Homecoming"*, New York: Grove Press, 1971.

Monographs

Katherine H. Burkman, *The Dramatic World of Harold Pinter: its Basis in Ritual*, Columbus, Ohio: Ohio State U.P., 1971.

Martin Esslin, *The Peopled Wound: the Plays of Harold Pinter*, London: Methuen, and New York: Doubleday, 1970.

Lois G. Gordon, *Stratagems to Uncover Nakedness: the Dramas of Harold Pinter*. Columbia, Missouri: University of Missouri Press, 1969 [Literary Frontiers Series].

Ronald Hayman, *Harold Pinter*, London: Heinemann Educational Books, 1968 [Contemporary Playwrights Series].

Arnold P. Hinchliffe, *Harold Pinter*, New York: Twayne Publishers, 1967 [Twayne English Authors Series].

James R. Hollis, *Harold Pinter: the Poetics of Silence*, Carbondale, Illinois: Southern Illinois U.P., 1970.

Walter Kerr, *Harold Pinter*, New York and London: Columbia U.P., 1967 [Columbia Essays on Modern Writers].

Alrene Sykes, *Harold Pinter*, St Lucia: Queensland U.P., and New York: Humanities Press, 1970.

John Russell Taylor, *Harold Pinter*, Harlow: Longmans, for the British Council, 1969 [Writers and Their Work Series].

CRITICAL AND GENERAL STUDIES

Victor E. Amend, "Harold Pinter: Some Credits and Debits", *Modern Drama*, X, 1967, 165–74.

Arthur Ashworth, "New Theatre: Ionesco, Beckett, Pinter", *Southerly*, XXII, 1962, 145–52.

F. J. Bernhard, "Beyond Realism: the Plays of Harold Pinter", *Modern Drama*, VIII, 1965, 185–91.

James T. Boulton, "Harold Pinter: *The Caretaker* and Other Plays", *Modern Drama*, VI, 1963, 131–40.

J. J. Bray, "The Ham Funeral", *Meanjin*, XXI, March 1962, 32–4.

Adrian Brine, "Mac Davies is no Clochard", *Drama*, LVI, Summer 1961, 35–7.

John Russell Brown, "Mr Pinter's Shakespeare", *Critical Quarterly*, V, 1963, 251–65.

John Russell Brown, "Dialogue in Pinter and Others", *Critical Quarterly*, VII, 1965, 225–43.

Ronald Bryden, "Three Men in a Room" and "A Stink of Pinter" in *The Unfinished Hero*, London: Faber and Faber, 1969, 86–90 and 91–5.

Katherine Burkman, "Pinter's *A Slight Ache* as Ritual", *Modern Drama*, XI, 1968, 326–35.

Nicholas Canaday, Jr., "Harold Pinter's *Tea Party*: Seeing and Non-Seeing", *Studies in Short Fiction*, VI, 1969, 580–5.

Mark Cohen, "The Plays of Harold Pinter", *Jewish Quarterly*, VIII, Summer 1961, 21–2.

Ruby Cohn, "The World of Harold Pinter", *Tulane Drama Review*, VI, iii, 1962, 55–68.

Ruby Cohn, "Latter Day Pinter", *Drama Survey*, III, 1964, 367–77.

Ruby Cohn, "The Absurdly Absurd: Avatars of Godot", *Comparative Literature*, II, 1965, 233–40.

David Cook and Harold F. Brooks, "A Room with Three Views: Harold Pinter's *The Caretaker*", *Komos*, I, 1967, 62–9.

Nigel Dennis, "Pintermania", *New York Review of Books*, 17th December 1970, 21–2.

Earl J. Dias, "The Enigmatic World of Harold Pinter", *Drama Critique*, XI, Fall 1968, 119–24.

Kay Dick, "Pinter and the Fearful Matter", *Texas Quarterly*, IV, 1961, 257–65.

Denis Donoghue, "London Letter: Moral West End", *Hudson Review*, XIV, Spring 1961, 93–103.

Bernard F. Dukore, "The Theatre of Harold Pinter", *Tulane Drama Review*, VI, iii, 1962, 43–54.

Bernard F. Dukore, "A Woman's Place", *Quarterly Journal of Speech*, LII, 1966, 237–41.

Martin Esslin, "Pinter and the Absurd", *Twentieth Century*, CLXIX, 1961, 176–85.

Martin Esslin, "Parallels and Proselytes: Harold Pinter", in *The Theatre of the Absurd*, London: Eyre and Spottiswoode, 1962, 205–23.

Martin Esslin, "Godot and His Children: the Theatre of Samuel Beckett and Harold Pinter", in *Experimental Drama*, ed. William A. Armstrong, London: Bell, 1963, 128–46.

Martin Esslin, "Pinter Translated", *Encounter*, XXX, iii, 1968, 45–7.

Gareth Lloyd Evans, "Pinter's Black Magic", in *The Curtain Rises: an Anthology of International Theatre*, comp. Dick Richards, London: Frewin, 1966, 68–72.

John Fletcher, "Harold Pinter, Rolland Dubillard and Eugene Ionesco", *Caliban*, III, ii, 1967, 149–52.

Abraham N. Franzblau, "A Psychiatrist Looks at *The Homecoming*", *Saturday Review*, 8th April 1967, 58.

William J. Free, "Treatment of Character in Harold Pinter's *The Homecoming*", *South Atlantic Bulletin*, XXXIV, November 1969, 1–5.

Kent G. Gallagher, "Harold Pinter's Dramaturgy", *Quarter Journal of Speech*, LII, 1966, 242–8.

Arthur Ganz, "A Clue to the Pinter Puzzle: the Triple Self in *The Homecoming*", *Educational Theatre Journal*, XXI, May 1969, 180–7.

Harry M. Geduld, "The Trapped Heroes of Harold Pinter", *Humanist*, XXVIII, March–April 1968, 24 ff.

Florence Jeanne Goodman, "Pinter's *The Caretaker: The Lower Depths* Descended", *Midwest Quarterly*, V, 1964, 117–26.

Stuart Hall, "Home Sweet Home", *Encore*, XII, July–August 1965, 30–4.

Patrick Henry, "Acting the Absurd", *Drama Critique*, VI, Winter 1963, 9–19

Martin Hilsky, "The Two Worlds of Harold Pinter's Plays", in *Prague Studies in English*, ed. Bohumil Trnka and Zdenek Stribrny, Prague: Caroline University, 1968.

Arnold Hinchliffe, "Mr Pinter's Belinda", *Modern Drama*, XI, 1968, 173–9

Jacqueline Hoefer, "Pinter and Whiting: Two Attitudes Towards the Alienated Artist", *Modern Drama*, IV, 1962, 402–8.

Catherine Hughes, "Pinter Is as Pinter Does", *Catholic World*, CCX, December 1969, 124–6.

Patrick Hutchings, "The Humanism of a Dumb Waiter", *Westerly*, I, 1963, 56–63.

John Kershaw, "Harold Pinter: Dramatist" and "Language and Communication", in *The Present Stage*, London: Collins, 1966, 70–8 and 79–87.

Francis L. Kunkel, "The Dystopia of Harold Pinter", *Renascence*, XXI, Autumn 1968, 17–20.

John Lahr, "Pinter and Chekhov: the Bond of Naturalism", *Tulane Drama Review*, XIII, ii, 1968, 137–45.

John Lahr, "Pinter the Spaceman", *Evergreen Review*, XII, No. 55, 1968, 49–52.

Clifford Leech, "Two Romantics: Arnold Wesker and Harold Pinter", in *Contemporary Theatre*, ed. John Russell Brown and Bernard Harris, London: Arnold, 1962, Stratford-upon-Avon Studies IV, 11–31.

Charles Marowitz, "Pinterism is Maximum Tension Through Minimum Information", *New York Times Magazine*, 1st October 1967, 36.

Gerald Mast, "Pinter's *Homecoming*", *Drama Survey*, VI, 1968, 266–77.

Valerie Minogue, "Taking Care of the Caretaker", *Twentieth Century*, CLXVIII, 1960, 243–8.

Kelly Morris, "*The Homecoming*", *Tulane Drama Review*, XI, ii, 1966, 185–91.

Kristin Morrison, "Pinter and the New Irony", *Quarterly Journal of Speech*, LV, 1969, 388–93.

Gerald Nelson, "Harold Pinter Goes to the Movies", *Chicago Review*, XIX, 1966, 33–43.

Hugh Nelson, "*The Homecoming*: Kith and Kin", in *Modern British Dramatists*, ed. John Russell Brown, Englewood Cliffs, New Jersey: Prentice-Hall, 1968.

Ray Orley, "Pinter and Menace", *Drama Critique*, XI, Fall 1968, 125–48.

John Pesta, "Pinter's Usurpers", *Drama Survey*, VI, 1967, 54–65.

Richard Schechner, "Puzzling Pinter", *Tulane Drama Review*, XI, iii, 1966, 176–84.

Claire Sprague, "Possible or Necessary?" *New Theatre Magazine*, VIII, i, 1967, 36–7.

Bert O. States, "Pinter's *Homecoming*: the Shock of Non-Recognition", *Hudson Review*, XXI, 1968, 474–86.

R. F. Storch, "Harold Pinter's Happy Families", *Massachusetts Review*, VIII, 1967, 703–12.

Alrene Sykes, "Harold Pinter's *Dwarfs*", *Komos*, I, 1967, 70–5.

John Russell Taylor, "A Room and Some Views", in *Anger and After*, second edition, London: Methuen, 1969, 321–59.

Peter C. Thornton, "Blindness and the Confrontation with Death: Three Plays by Harold Pinter", *Die Neueren Sprachen*, XVII, 1968, 212–13.

Augusta Walker, "Messages from Pinter", Modern Drama, X, 1967, 1–10.

Irving Wardle, "There's Music in that Room", in *The Encore Reader*, ed. Charles Marowitz *et al.*, London: Methuen, 1965, 129–32.

Irving Wardle, "*The Birthday Party*", in *The Encore Reader*, ed. Charles Marowitz *et al.*, London: Methuen, 1965, 76–8.

George E. Wellwarth, "Harold Pinter: the Comedy of Allusiveness", in *The Theater of Protest and Paradox*, New York: New York U.P., 1964, 197–211.

Raymond Williams, "*The Birthday Party*", in *Drama from Ibsen to Brecht*, London: Chatto and Windus, 1968, 322–5.